The Silver Medalist

The Silver Medalist

T.J. Blackley

To Riki,
Tessbook! ♡
Love, TJB

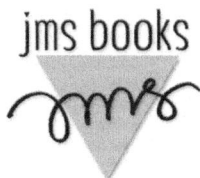

jms books

THE SILVER MEDALIST

All Rights Reserved © 2022 by T.J. Blackley

JMS Books LLC
PO Box 234
Colonial Heights, VA 23834
www.jms-books.com

Printed in the United States of America

ISBN: 9798834358213

To Rae, without whom nothing would get written.

*This book couldn't have been made without The Mad Hatters,
the loveliest and queerest community on the Internet.
Thanks especially to Kaz, IA, Riki, and all the Creative Hellions!*

And, of course, much love to Pickles, the best cat in the world.

Chapter 1

IT'S OVER, DANNY realizes as the cameras flash, and he smiles to match them, holding his gold medal up to his face. He's sixteen, his Juniors figure skating career is over, and he's ended it on top, with a World Championship gold medal. He's done it.

His coach meets him at the boards when the photo op is over, grinning as Danny skates toward him. "Well done," he says, holding out his hand formally. Danny shakes it, still beaming. "I'll be excited to see what you do under Coach Hartmann in Seniors," the man goes on. "I expect great things from you, Danny."

"I won't let you down," Danny promises. "Can I take a shower now? I put on way too much hairspray this morning and I'm starting to get light-headed." Coach Friedl laughs and leads him out of the rink, right into the crowd of press that stand between them and the outside world.

A couple of interviews later, the two of them manage to escape the crowd and leave the building. It's March in Germany, so the air is bitingly crisp, and Danny tilts his face into the wind. It feels like he's skating again, the cold air of the rink rushing past him as he flies across the ice. There's no better feeling in the world, and he sighs happily, despite his coach's grumbling.

The hotel is a few blocks from the rink, and he and his coach walk in silence. Coach Friedl has been good for him over the past few years, drawing out his potential, but he only coaches Juniors and below. He's the one who introduced Danny to his next coach, Nico Hartmann, at the start of this past season. "You'll want this one," Danny heard Friedl murmur to the Seniors coach. "He's going to go far." Danny has kept that locked in his chest ever since.

To his surprise, there's a figure lurking in the shadows by the hotel entrance. Danny squints at it as they approach, and whoever it is steps out of the darkness, light glinting off their—his—shiny blond hair. It's Andrei Lebed, Danny realizes with a lurch. The Yellow Swan of Russia, who graduated to Seniors two years ago despite being only a year older than Danny, two seasons' worth of Juniors gold under his belt and already a decent amount of Seniors gold too. What is he doing *here*?

"Daniel Schaer!" he calls out, lifting a hand.

"You know me?" Danny manages, freezing in his tracks.

Andrei laughs and steps toward him. "Of course," he says, shoving his hands in his pockets with a shiver. He nods to Friedl and turns back to Danny. "I wanted to say congratulations on your win today," he goes on. "Your triple flip is quite good."

It's Danny's signature move. He blushes to the roots of his dark hair. "Thanks," he says. "I'll have quads soon." Andrei is famous for, among other things, landing the quadruple toe loop at just thirteen, and he's added the quad Salchow this past season.

"You'd better," Andrei says, giving him a mock-stern look. "I expect you to be a proper competitor when you hit Seniors. Are you moving up next season?" Danny nods. "Good," Andrei declares. "No point hanging around what you've already conquered, I always say."

"Really?" Danny says, unable to shut his mouth. "You *always* say that?"

Andrei barks out a surprised laugh. "No," he admits ruefully, "but I should. It's catchy. Well, I won't keep you," he adds, rocking back on his heels. "Just wanted to say congratulations."

"Thanks," Danny says again. "See you in Seniors." Andrei flashes him a grin and they part ways, Danny and his coach into the hotel and Andrei away from it.

"You've made your first friend in Seniors already," Coach Friedl remarks.

Danny shakes his head. "Andrei was just being nice."

"'Being nice' is what friends *means*, Danny," his coach says teasingly. Danny just rolls his eyes, grinning, and heads for the shower. His costume is starting to itch.

His parents are appropriately thrilled with his victory when he calls them afterward, his father cheering so loudly in the background of the call that Danny knows they'll get a noise complaint from their neighbors in the morning. "Thanks," he says when he can get a word in edgewise. "I'm really proud of myself."

"We're proud of you too, sweetheart," his mother says. Then, of course: "Have you done your homework?"

"Moooooom," he groans. "I just won the *World Championships*, and you want me to write an *essay?*"

"Yes," she says sternly. "If you don't have at least an outline by the time you get home, we won't put your medal up in your cupboard."

That's a lie and they both know it, but he just sighs and says, "Fine. I'll do it on the plane, even though I *should* be sleeping because I'm a *growing boy* and I need all my rest, but I'll stay awake and do my *essay* instead, and never mind what it does to my growth." She's laughing by the time he's done, and he grins. "Love you, Mom."

"Love you, too, Danny."

"Love you, son!" his father hollers. Danny shouts his love back and hangs up, slipping his feet into the soft slippers he packs for competitions and padding out of the room in search of a vending machine.

He manages to finish the whole outline on the flight back to Bern the next day, *and* half the writing too, and his father hangs his medal up with its fellows with pride, taking a cloth to it until it shines.

The contract from Coach Hartmann arrives the next day, couriered over from his office at the rink, in a crisp white envelope. "You're sure?" Danny's mother asks him, pen hovering over the paper.

"I'm sure," Danny says firmly. She signs, and then he signs, and then it's really done. His Juniors career is over, his Seniors career about to begin. They slip the papers back into the envelope and the courier gets back on his bike to ferry the signed contract back to the rink.

The rest of the school year is almost an anticlimax, after that. His friends are all congratulatory, and Simon in particular clasps him in a close hug, which makes him shiver with something unknown and thrilling, but none of his teachers seem to care. He passes his essay, which is something, and manages to scrape together good enough grades to pass the year completely.

His classmates throw a rager once the year is officially over, but for Danny, the real work is just beginning. As soon as Danny texts him that his schoolwork is over for the summer, Nico Hartmann schedules a time to bring him into the rink to meet his new rinkmates and set up an off-season training schedule.

Danny spends long enough in front of his mirror that morning that his mother has to shout up the stairs that he's about to be late. The rink is far enough away that it makes a decent workout at a run, but he's not officially training today, so he takes his bike, locking it up at the rack outside the front door and taking a moment to shake his clothing straight again and pat down his hair.

Nico meets him just inside, a round, squat, jovial man with a shiny bald head, blue glasses, and a whiff of cologne even from a few feet away. "Nervous?" he asks knowingly, and laughs when Danny frowns at him. "Come on, they don't bite," he says, putting an arm around Danny's shoulders and steering him toward the rink proper.

"Normally everyone has separate practice times during the summer," Nico says, "but I schedule a group one at the start of every off-season to reevaluate training regimes and introduce new people. So most of them you won't see very often." Danny nods, jamming his hands in his pockets to keep from fidgeting, and they go through the doors, the bite of the chilled air instantly calming him down. The rink is relatively full, half a dozen skaters working individually or in pairs. They're all skilled, Danny notes, and he quails a little bit at the thought.

Nico calls over the pairs skaters first—he introduces them as Nolan and Emma Rohner, a sibling pair in their early twenties, with matching dark brown hair and twinkling eyes. "Great job at Worlds!" Nolan says. "Killer step sequence in your free skate."

"Thanks," Danny says shyly, and they wave and zoom off back to the far side of the rink.

Nico also has two ladies singles skaters under his tutelage, Malea Rossi and Mira Walker. Mira is about Nolan and Emma's age, light red hair and freckles, but Malea is closer to Danny's; he remembers her senior debut two years ago and is able to compliment her on a Grand Prix Final bronze medal from last season, which makes her beam at him. She's a bright one, shiny blond hair almost the same shade as Andrei Lebed's, and sparkling white teeth when she smiles. Taken all together, she makes Danny's eyes ache like looking at the sun, but she's nice enough when she welcomes him to the rink. "She has that effect on everyone," Nico murmurs when the ladies skate away. Danny laughs.

"And now, my ice dancers," Nico says, signaling to the last pair on the ice. "I admit I don't usually take ice dancers, but I've made an exception for these two." The pair make their way over to where Nico and Danny are standing, and Danny feels his heart stutter in his chest.

The girl is pretty, dark skin and darker hair slicked back from her face in a tight ponytail. She grins and waves at him, sliding into the boards with a practiced glide that Danny takes a moment to distantly envy. But it's the boy that catches Danny's eye, tall and broad-shouldered, maybe two years older than Danny, with wavy light brown hair cascading down from his head and a crooked smile. "Noemi Tanner and Noah Favre," Nico introduces them. "This is Danny Schaer, our newest member of the rink."

"Welcome," Noemi says brightly. "I saw your free program at the Junior Worlds; it was really amazing."

"Thanks," Danny manages, tearing his eyes away from Noah. "I hope I'm good enough for Seniors."

"Nico'll whip you into shape," Noah says airily. "He's a good coach."

"Damning me with faint praise, I see, Noah," Nico says drily, and Noah laughs. Danny's heart stutters again.

"Welcome to the rink," Noah says, turning back to Danny. "If you have any questions about anything, just find me or Noemi and we'll help you."

"Do you have a cell phone?" Noemi asks. Danny nods, patting his pocket where the sturdy flip phone is safely stowed. "Give him our numbers, Nico," she says to their coach, who nods. "Call or text us anytime," she tells Danny. "I'm glued to my phone. When I'm not practicing," she adds quickly, with a nervous glance at Nico.

"Nice save," the coach says. "Alright, back to it, you two." The ice dancers wave again and skate back to their spot on the ice. "That's everyone," Nico says. "You'll fit in splendidly."

"I hope so," Danny says. "Everyone seems nice."

"For the most part they are," Nico says. "And like I said, you probably won't see much of them until the season starts and you get more ice time. But for now, we have some paperwork to go over."

Danny follows him over to his little office off the rink and fills out form after form. "We'll make you an appointment with our nutritionist," Nico says, "but I wouldn't worry too much about that. I talked with your last coach and the regime you were on should be just fine to continue."

"Okay." Danny signs his name on the last form.

"Last thing." Nico scribbles on a sticky note and passes it across the desk. "Noah and Noemi's cell numbers and emails," he says as Danny takes it. "I hope you take them up on their offer. They've both been with me for several years and know the ropes well by now."

"I will," Danny promises, folding the sticky note and slipping it into his pocket alongside his phone. "Good." Nico puts his hands flat on the desk and stands up. "That's all for today, I think. I'll see you back here next Tuesday for some solo ice time. Keep up with your workouts and your diet until then." He looks at Danny over his glasses. "I'll know if you slack off."

"Yes, sir," Danny says, standing.

"And no *sir*," Nico adds, smiling to take the sting out. "I'm Nico, or Coach if you have to be formal." Danny nods. "I'll walk you out," Nico says, and does, lingering by the door until Danny unlocks his bike and straddles it. "Enjoy your break from school," he calls. Danny waves and sets off for home again.

"How was it?" his father asks when Danny gets home.

"Fine." Danny flops down on the couch next to him. "Everyone seems nice."

"Good," his father booms. "I'd hate to have to go down there and start cracking heads when we've only just signed the paperwork." Danny laughs and steals the remote from him.

Chapter 2

NICO, NATURALLY, HAS high expectations for all his skaters, and Danny has a long way to go from Juniors-ready to Seniors-ready, so he spends most of the summer training and conditioning, alternating between the gym and the rink. Nico puts him in touch with his trainer, who helps him come up with a regime that will get him in shape without overtaxing his still-growing muscles.

At the rink, he and Nico spend their time refining his elements, his triple-rotation jumps and spins and steps. Under Nico's careful eye and a harness, Danny also starts training the quadruple toe loop, the easier of the two quad jumps that exist at the moment. He's wanted it for *ages* but Coach Friedl wouldn't let him try it, and even Nico is reluctant, Danny still being as young as he is. He lands it without the harness for the first time in late June and Nico hugs him hard in celebration and, for the first time, drops the c-word.

"I generally let my older and more experienced skaters have a sizable say in their choreographies," he tells Danny, arms folded as Danny unlaces his boots after practice that day. "For skaters as young as you, though, I usually choreograph them myself. How does that sound?"

"Fine," Danny says, stowing his skates in his bag and tugging on his sneakers. "I trust you."

"Good," Nico says. "I have some ideas for your programs this season. We'll leave the question of the quad toe loop open for now; if you're more consistent by August, then we'll talk about putting it in your programs. Deal?"

"Deal," Danny says, standing and picking up his bag. "Thanks."

"Gym tomorrow," Nico says. "Have fun and be safe."

Despite it being summer, he still has schoolwork to deal with, summer reading and science methodologies and math problem sets. "I feel like we never see you anymore," Simon complains one day over ice cream, picking a sprinkle off his cone and chucking it at Danny. "You're always busy skating."

Danny picks the sprinkle off his cheek and eats it. "It's my career," he says, making Ella roll her eyes and gag. He grins at her before turning back to Simon. "But I'm sorry. I'll try to make more time for you guys."

"You can start by coming over and helping me with the biology reading," Simon says, taking a bite out of his cone. "I don't understand it at all."

"What makes you think I do?" Danny points out. Simon just turns those bright blue eyes on him, a slight pout to his lips, and Danny sighs. "Fine. I'll come over after skating tomorrow."

"Can I come too?" Ella wheedles. "I'm going to fail that class, I can already tell."

"You've never failed a class in your life," Simon says. "But fine, come over too. We'll have a study group." He catches Danny's eye, a conspiratorial *oh well* tilt to his mouth that makes Danny's stomach squirm.

Study groups with Danny's friends are always a riot but rarely end with actual work getting done, so he goes home the next day just as confused as he had been at the start. Pulling out his cell phone, he sends a message to Noemi for help.

Danny: Are you any good at biology?

Noemi: Ha! No

Noemi: Noah is, though

Noemi: Ask him

Danny: Okay, thanks

❖

DANNY: I NEED help

Noah: With what?

Danny: The Krebs cycle

Danny: Noemi says you're good at biology

Noah: I'm decent

Noah: Can I call you? Too long an explanation for text

Danny: Sure

Danny somehow manages to focus enough on the lesson, despite getting a little lost in Noah's Teacher Voice, that he actually understands it. "Thank you," he says fervently, scribbling the last notes onto his paper. "You're a lifesaver."

Noah laughs. "Anytime, Danny."

"I have to go call all my friends and explain it to them now that I understand it. Thank you," Danny repeats. "I'll give you all the credit."

"Don't bother," Noah says. "Make yourself look good, I don't mind."

"You're the best," Danny declares, and they say goodbye and hang up. Danny dials Simon next. "I understand it," he says as soon as the other boy picks up, and launches into an explanation of the Krebs cycle.

"Crap, crap, slow down, let me get my notebook," Simon cuts over him. Danny can hear the rustling of paper and the click of a pen. "How'd you figure it out?"

"I'm a genius."

"Obviously," Simon drawls. "But seriously, you were just as confused as me and Ella two hours ago."

Danny fiddles with a loose thread on his bedspread. "I had a friend explain it to me." He hopes it's not too presumptuous to call Noah a friend at this point, but somehow he doesn't think the other boy would mind.

"Another friend, huh?" Simon asks. "Are you cheating on us? Should I be jealous?"

"Absolutely be jealous," Danny says, grinning. "Are you ready yet?"

"Yes, yes, go ahead."

Despite all the work he's putting in, the summer slips by, and all too soon the specter of Grand Prix assignments starts looming large. The Grand Prix of Figure Skating is a series of six competitions of skaters from all over the world; the top six skaters in each division—men's singles, ladies singles, pair skating, and ice dancing—are selected to compete at the Grand Prix Final in early December. It's one of the most prestigious events in the figure skating season.

Danny medaled at Junior Worlds, so he's guaranteed one assignment in the Grand Prix series. He'd need two to get to the Final, but that's alright; a guaranteed one is more than a lot of early-career skaters get. And it's a lot less pressure, knowing the Final is off the table from the start this year.

Of course, there's the added pressure of it being one of the only events he'll be skating in this season, aside from Nationals and maybe Worlds, so it kind of cancels out.

Assignments come out in mid-August, just after Danny's seventeenth birthday. Danny makes his mother look, his fists pressed to his mouth in stress. "It's the Bompard," she says finally, and Danny lets out a long breath. The Trophée Éric Bompard, the fourth event in the series. He's going to Paris.

His other rinkmates all have events too, two each. They're all scattered throughout the other five events, though; Danny will be going to Paris alone, just Nico by his side.

There's a press conference after the assignments; there always is, and Danny has been before, as a Juniors skater. He's small potatoes now that he's in Seniors, though, and he doesn't have to say much, just sit there in his suit and try and look impressive. Nico ruffles his hair when it's over and tells him he did well.

Once the assignments are out, it's the school year's turn to loom large over Danny's mind. There's a party beforehand, of course; there's always a party before school starts. Danny uses his widening shoulders to justify a shopping spree and turns up in new clothes that fit like a dream, even if it is just for the moment. Ella teases him for twenty minutes before someone breaks out the alcohol, but Simon just gives him an appreciative smile and a slug on the bicep.

The alcohol at these parties is always *terrible*, but Danny gamely downs two cups in pursuit of dancing. He loses Ella at some point, and Simon isn't dancing, but there are plenty of other people on the floor, and he drifts for a long stretch of time to the throbbing beat and the heat of other people, until a hand closes around his wrist.

It's Simon, pulling him off the combination living-room-and-dance-floor and into a quiet corner. "I've got to tell you something," he shouts in Danny's ear over the music. "Can we talk?"

"Sure!" Danny shouts back, and follows when Simon leads him out of the living room and down a hallway.

He's a little surprised when Simon leads him to a closet, but he's a little drunk and it's nicely metaphorical, so he just goes in and shifts aside a bit to make room for Simon to close the door.

"So," Danny says, their knees pressing together and Simon's breath on his cheek. "What did you want to tell me?"

Simon sighs. "We're moving away," he says, all in a rush. "My family. My parents got new jobs and we're moving away in December."

Danny's stomach drops to about his knees and he nods. "I see. We'll miss you, me and Ella. The lunch table won't be the same without you."

"It's not *Ella* I want to miss me," Simon murmurs. Danny leans back and looks at him. "I didn't just drag you in here to tell you that," Simon confesses. His eyes are wide and he's sweating a little. Danny raises an eyebrow. "Don't kill me if I've got this wrong," Simon says, and he lifts his hands and puts them on either side of Danny's face. "I'm moving away in four months, so this is my last chance to do this," and he pulls Danny's face forward and presses their mouths together.

It's Danny's first kiss, and it confirms a number of things Danny has always known about himself but never really *known*, not practically. Simon tastes like the party's terrible alcohol and also kind of like pot, and Danny licks it off his lips when his friend pulls back. "Did I get it wrong?" Simon whispers.

Eyes still shut, Danny shakes his head. "Nope, not wrong. Not wrong at all."

"Oh, thank Christ," and then they're kissing again, and Danny gets the rest of his body involved, his knees pressing a little farther between Simon's and his hands going to Simon's waist. Simon works Danny's mouth open, and he must have done this before, or read some *very explicit* books, and Danny will winkle the stories out of him later but for now he takes Simon's nervous tongue into his mouth and lets out a sound he didn't know he was capable of making.

He finds himself hard faster than he's ever gotten hard in his life, and he's a seventeen-year-old boy, so that's saying something. "Do you wanna," he whispers, biting Simon's lip and letting one hand slip around to rest on his lower back.

"*Christ*, yeah," Simon swears again. They fumble blindly at each other's trousers, still kissing, and Danny lets out a hiss as Simon yanks his fly down and his fingers graze Danny's cock, already half-hard and growing. Simon whimpers, and Danny tears his mouth away to focus on what his fingers are doing and finally gets his friend's zipper down, then pushes his trousers and boxers to mid-thigh.

Simon whines as Danny touches him, high-pitched drones that go straight to Danny's balls, almost more than Simon's reciprocating fingers do. Simon's free hand tangles in his hair, fingers catching on a snarl and tugging, and the sharp burst of almost-pain sends Danny over the edge, spilling over Simon's wrist and the fabric of his own briefs with a bitten-off cry.

He somehow manages to keep working Simon through it, and the other boy finishes before he's fully come back to himself. They pant against each other for a few minutes, until Simon reaches to a shelf above Danny's head and comes back with a washcloth to clean their hands.

"Is this how you expected this conversation to go?" Danny asks with a grin, working his trousers back up over his hips.

Simon grins back. "It was the best-case scenario."

Danny laughs and throws his arms around Simon's shoulders, pulling him in for another kiss. "We'll do this again?" he murmurs.

Simon nods, rubbing his nose against Danny's. "It's only four months, but I bet we can have some fun before I have to leave."

Danny feels himself grin, sharp as a blade. "No doubt."

Simon leaves first, promising to knock on the door when five minutes have passed and it's safe for Danny to come out. He spends the time with his eyes closed, thinking hard.

His parents have always taught him that sex doesn't change a person, that virginity is a social construct, but he does feel… *different*, somehow. More settled into his skin, more present in his body. He can feel long-held muscle tension loosening, as though his orgasm had wrung his whole body out and left him limp and loose. He likes it.

Ella shouts at them for running off when they make it back to the living room. "I had no one to dance with!" she scolds, one hand around each of their wrists to tow them after her. "It was *horrible*."

Danny shares a laughing glance with Simon, then sweeps Ella back onto the dance floor.

Chapter 3

DANNY WINDS UP calling on Noah's help in biology a handful more times as the school semester kicks off. He tries his best to time his texts and calls to when he knows Noah will be at practice so he can just leave a message and Noah can call him back when he's ready, but Noah picks up half the time anyway, and he always has the time to help.

Danny drags Simon and Ella through biology in his wake, despite their ever-more-vocal curiosity about his mysterious tutor friend. "Are they prettier than me?" Ella asks after one study group, nervously patting her hair.

"Are they prettier than *me*?" Simon demands, mirroring her movements. Danny just laughs at them and turns back to his textbook. Best to keep the streams of Simon and Noah, at least, uncrossed, he thinks.

The Grand Prix series starts in October, and everyone at the rink gets much, much busier come late September, to the point where Danny is often sharing rink time with the others. For the most part, Nico keeps them on opposite sides of the rink, but every now and then Danny gets lucky and Nico will assign someone to mentor him in some skill or other.

Under Mira's tutelage, his spins get better than they've ever been. Nico is always free with his smiles and praise, but Danny can tell when he's really impressed the man, and the camel spin in his free program halfway through October is one of those times.

His favorite mentorships, though, are when he gets to work with Noemi on his extensions. Danny has a bad habit of marking his movements instead of fully extending them, and apparently Noemi is the best in the rink at countering that impulse. Nico actually pulls her in alone for one of Danny's solo sessions to work on it.

"So, you and Noah," Danny says during their water break, leaning back against the boards and catching his breath. "How did you two meet?"

"Oh, Nico introduced us," she says, wiping her brow on her sweatband. "He's had Noah since Novices, and he knows my ballet teacher and pulled me from her class when I was eleven. I think he was disappointed when we decided on dance together; he wanted us for pairs, I think."

"Why did you pick dance?" Danny asks.

She shrugs. "It just suited our styles better. Besides, I'm not one for jumps, and neither is Noah."

"Makes sense," Danny says, rubbing his knee where it still aches from the morning's quad toe loop drills. "Are you two…"

Noemi cackles. "Oh *God*, no," she says, and pats his shoulder. "We play it up for the programs, but no, nothing like that."

Danny nods, trying not to let his relief show on his face. He's not even sure why he's relieved, really; he's with Simon for a couple more months, and even if he weren't, there's no indication Noah would be interested in *him* even if he isn't dating Noemi.

He must not do a very good job, though, because Noemi slings an arm around his shoulders conspiratorially. "It's the hair, isn't it?" she whispers. "It's magical."

Danny shakes himself. "It's fine," he says. "Shall we get back to it?"

"Sure thing," she tells him, a frown flickering across her face. He sets his water bottle on the boards and skates back out to their spot on the ice. She runs him through his step sequences a few more times before declaring to Nico that he's doing much better. "All credit to me, of course."

"Of course," Nico says with an indulgent smile. "Alright, Danny, run through your full short for me." Danny does, downgrading his jumps to single rotations due to how tired he is but putting his all into the extensions and steps. "Good," Nico says when he's finished, doubled over with his hands on his knees and panting. "I'm satisfied with where you are. Starting next week we'll build some contingencies for missed jumps. You need to have backup plans already as muscle memory when you compete."

"Yes, Nico," Danny says. "Can I go stretch now?"

"Off with you."

Instead of going to stretch right away, though, he pulls Noemi aside, taking her by the elbow and tugging them both behind the bleachers. She comes willingly, but when he turns to face her, she's frowning again. "What's up?" she asks, crossing her arms.

Danny opens his mouth and shuts it again, a little at a loss. "How..." he starts, having to pause to swallow. "How did you know?" he finally asks, voice very quiet.

Her face goes a little soft and understanding. "Oh, Danny," she says, putting a hand on his arm. "Let's just say you're not my only gay friend."

"Don't tell Noah," he begs. "I don't want him to know."

"Okay, okay," she says, reaching up to squeeze his shoulder. "Don't worry, I won't tell him. Although I guarantee you, one hundred percent, he will be fine with it."

"Really?" She nods, smiling reassuringly. "Still," Danny says. "I'm not ready yet."

"That's fine," she tells him with another squeeze to his shoulder. "I'm sorry for putting you on the spot like that. I didn't realize, but I should have thought first."

"It's okay." Danny manages a smile. "I'm glad you're okay with it."

"Totally, totally okay with it," she assures him. "And my lips are sealed."

"Can I hug you?" She laughs and folds him in a warm embrace, ruffling his hair. "Thanks," he says when she releases him. "Let's go stretch now."

"You got it, champ."

Somehow, the next few weeks disappear, and then it's mid-November and the Bompard is right around the corner. Four days before their flight, Nico calls Danny into his office. "Shut the door," he directs, sitting down. Danny does so and drops into the chair opposite him. "I want you to know, I'm not singling you out," Nico says, and Danny's stomach twists. "I give this talk to all my skaters before their first international competition. You're not going to enjoy it, but it's important."

"Is this the part where you tell me I'm a small fish about to be in a huge pond, and not to get my hopes up?" Danny asks, his mouth dry. He's been working hard to keep his expectations low, really he has, but sometimes the excitement of his *first Seniors Grand Prix event* is just too much.

"What?" Nico blinks at him, and then his face crinkles in understanding. "Oh, no, lad, nothing like that. Here, I'll just spit it out." He pulls two boxes from a drawer, setting them on his desk. One box is marked Ceylor, the other Coltene. Condoms and dental dams. Danny almost laughs with relief, but he doesn't want to have to explain that Nico is a little late for the safe sex talk.

"I don't want to go all your-body-is-a-temple on you," Nico says, pushing the boxes across the desk, "but you're a professional athlete, and you have to take care of yourself. I've seen too many skaters fall because they're not taking the proper precautions. I'm not here to judge you for what you do or don't choose to do around your skating; I'm just here to make sure you're being safe."

Now that the relief is passing, the embarrassment is starting to set in. Besides, Danny has a choice to make here, and an ever-shrinking window of time in which to make it. He looks at Nico's face, so carefully, studiously blank, and goes all in for bravery. He puts his hand on the box of dental dams and pushes it back across the desk. "I won't, uh, be needing these."

"I see," Nico says. Danny chances another look at his face, and he's smiling now, his most reassuring one. Danny relaxes a little, relief rushing through him. "Take them anyway," Nico suggests, pushing them back toward him. "They might come in handy."

Danny kind of really wants to ask how dental dams come in handy for gay men, but also he does *not* want to have that talk with his coach, so he stuffs both boxes into his skate bag. "I'll be safe," he makes himself say. "Anything else?"

Nico shakes his head. "You're done for the day." Danny flashes him a quick smile and flees.

The condoms, at least, come in handy sooner than Nico might have expected. The night before his flight to Paris, Simon comes over to farewell him in private.

Danny lets out a little whimper as Simon's teeth worry at the skin of his neck. "Don't leave a mark," he hisses, squirming under his friend.

"I *won't*," Simon says, kissing the spot and then licking it before moving further down. "You have to let that go."

"I'll let it go when my mother lets me coming home with a love bite," Danny says. Simon doesn't answer, just shifts his thigh further up between Danny's legs. Danny rocks into it with a sigh. "I really should be getting to sleep," he says, just to feel Simon's hands tighten where they're pinning his wrists to the bed. "I have a flight tomorrow."

"You have a flight at two in the afternoon tomorrow," Simon says into Danny's collarbone, "and I haven't gotten you off yet."

"Well, get to it." Danny hitches his hips up into Simon's again and the boy laughs.

"Impatient," he murmurs, shifting up to kiss Danny on the mouth. "How do you want it?"

"Mmm, I want your mouth."

Simon kisses his neck, feather-light and wet. "Do you now." He takes one hand off Danny's wrists to palm the bulging crotch of his trousers.

"Simon, please, you came *half an hour ago* and you've been torturing me ever since," Danny says in a voice that is only just barely not a whine. "Please touch me."

Simon kisses him again, deep and hard, and shifts his weight off him. "Alright, off." Danny scrambles to push his trousers and briefs down to mid-thigh while Simon fishes a condom out of Danny's new box and passes it to him. Danny rolls it on, pushing himself back against the pillows, and Simon crawls into position and leans down to slip his lips around Danny's cock.

"Oh fuck," Danny hisses, his fingers tightening in the sheets as Simon starts to suck him. "Oh shit, yes, *ahhhhh...*" Simon gazes up at him, bright blue eyes glittering, smirking as much as he can with his mouth full. "Oh fuck," Danny whispers again, more than a little lost in his friend's gaze. "God, you're so *hot*, Simon."

Simon pulls off to say, "That means a lot, coming from you, Danny." Danny whimpers at the praise and Simon returns to his task, cheeks hollowing as he sucks and sucks, tongue pressed flat against Danny's underside. Their first blow jobs were sloppy, toothy things, but Simon in particular has gotten *loads* better in the intervening two months.

"*Fuck*," Danny bites out as he starts to crest, hands moving from the sheets to scrabble at Simon's shoulders. "Almost, almost, *oh*, thank you, thank you..." He arches, back off the bed, until Simon has to throw an arm over his hips to hold him down, and that's a new and interesting delight that sends another shock through him.

Simon holds him in his mouth until he's done, and then pops off, rubbing his jaw. "Gorgeous," he proclaims, running his palm down Danny's abs, which are still quivering as he catches his breath.

Danny pushes himself up on one hand and catches Simon behind the head with the other, pulling him into a bruising kiss. "I really do have to sleep now," he murmurs against his lips, snickering when Simon pouts.

"Fine," Simon says, rolling off him in search of his boxers. "Jet off to your *international competition*, with positively *hordes* of nubile athletes to replace me with. I see how it is."

Danny grins, passing him a sock from the other side of the bed. Simon sits to pull it on, and Danny catches his chin in one hand. "I'm yours until December," he says seriously. "I promised, and I keep my promises."

"I wish it could be longer," Simon confesses, biting his lip.

"So do I," Danny says honestly. "But we still have some time. And I promise to think of you and only you when I jerk off in the hotel shower."

That makes Simon smile, which makes Danny smile, and they part with a kiss.

Chapter 4

DANNY'S PARENTS SEE him into Nico's car the next day, his father's big hand on his head and booming voice saying, "Be magnificent," staying with him long after he's buckled into his seat on the plane. The flight is only an hour and a half and he intends to do homework, but instead finds himself blinking awake as the plane lands in France.

"I hope this doesn't mean you were up all night," Nico murmurs sternly, but he smiles when Danny looks guiltily at him. "It's alright," he says, unbuckling himself to reach up for their bags. "You're young; you'll bounce back."

There's no one Danny knows competing at this event, so he does manage to get all his homework done in between public and private practice times. It's his first Grand Prix event in Seniors, so there are also plenty of interviews to get through; he thinks he does well enough, and Nico squeezes his shoulder with another smile when they're finally done.

He spends the morning of the short program stretching in the waiting area with the other skaters in his group, trying not to quail at all the talent packed into the space with him. Nico, ever the coach, just keeps pouring water into him and keeps him focused on the task at hand, which is loosening his hamstrings. "There's no one here but you that you have to care about," Nico says quietly. "Focus on yourself."

"If you don't think you can land the quad, don't do it," Nico goes on once he's rinkside and Danny is on the ice, quaking as the preceding skater gets his scores. "Put in the substitutes like we practiced if you have to."

"I can do it, Nico," Danny insists.

"Daniel." Danny looks at him. "Don't push yourself harder than you can take," Nico says, voice softer. "You have *time*, Danny, all the time in the world to achieve all you want to achieve. But you have to work your way up. You can't start at the top."

Danny swallows hard and nods. Nico pulls him into a warm hug over the boards, and then there's nothing left to do but head out.

They've placed the quad in his short program just at the end of the first half. If they were really trying to maximize points, they'd have put it in the latter half, since all elements in the second half of programs get a ten-percent points modifier, but Nico had said it was better to do it early, when he'd be less tired, and Danny had agreed, eventually. So there's one other jump and a step sequence before his big quad, and he manages to pull them all out to his satisfaction, which is a huge morale boost. He throws his all into the big jump.

He can tell as soon as he's in the air that he's not going to land it cleanly, but it isn't as bad as he fears in that swift moment; a hand on the ice, but he doesn't fall. He doesn't fall, and that's what he clings to for the rest of his performance, paying extra attention to his turnouts and extensions, trying to maximize his performance score to make up for the error.

Nico ruffles his hair in the kiss-and-cry while they wait for Danny's scores. "I'm proud of you," he says in Danny's ear.

"I didn't land it."

"But you didn't lose your head afterward. That's the mark of a great skater."

His score, when the announcer reads it out, is decent, in the high fifties despite his touchdown, and Danny's spirits rise a little as he goes through the post-performance interviews. Nico gives him his phone back eventually, and there are congratulatory messages waiting for him from his rinkmates, parents, and Ella and Simon.

It's only his first year in Seniors, so he hasn't had as much time as other skaters to garner big sponsorships, but he *did* win Worlds while in Juniors, so he has enough sponsorship money for his own room, thank God. He fulfills his promise to Simon before washing his hair and sinking into the bed to sleep like the dead.

Danny has two days off before he has to perform again, and he and Nico had struck a solemn deal when the schedule had been released. Danny spends the 16th of November holed up in his hotel room, studying like a mad thing between practices, and then on the 17th, Nico takes him sightseeing. He doesn't get to see that much of Paris, all told, the wait times at the Eiffel Tower being what they are, but the view from its high balcony is enough to sate him for now.

"You'll be here again," Nico tells him in the cab on the way back to the hotel. "You have a long Grand Prix future in front of you." Danny beams at him.

Men's singles free skate is on the 18th, a longer program than the first, and Danny has two quad toe loops scheduled, one in a combination jump in the first half. Nico doesn't warn him about them again, just gives him a look and then hugs him tight. "Go fly," he whispers.

Danny does. He touches down on the solo toe loop, but the combination jump is clean, and it's enough to propel him to a sixth-place finish overall, once all the other skaters have gone.

As he's tucking himself into bed that night, exhausted and happy, he notices a Facebook message from, surprisingly, Andrei Lebed.

Andrei: Well done

Danny: Thanks!

Danny: Wish I hadn't touched down on the solo, though

Andrei: Your form is clean

Andrei: You'll get there

Andrei: You'll be at the Final with me soon enough

Danny: I hope so

Noah and Noemi take him out to lunch when he gets home. It's a wonder they have time; they're in the run-up to the Final, poised to do well in their first time qualifying. "Are you nervous?" Danny asks them over grilled chicken and salad.

"No," Noah says, at the same time Noemi says, "Terrified." They laugh at each other. "Noah's brave," Noemi says, nudging him under the table. "I'm not."

"You're plenty brave," Noah says quietly, and she grins at him. "What about you?" he goes on, turning back to Danny. "Ready for Nationals?"

"I think so," Danny says. "Nervous, for sure, but my programs are in a good place. I just need to up my consistency on the damn quad toe loop."

"Best thing about ice dancing?" Noemi says. "No quads." Danny throws a spinach leaf at her and she cackles.

The next few weeks slip away from him, the only remarkable thing being the day Simon finds his prostate by accident. He reciprocates once he's recovered, of course, driving Simon to a twitchy orgasm into the condom in his mouth, two of Danny's fingers buried inside him. On the rink, Danny is back to landing the toe loop consistently, but Nico keeps him drilling it over and over in the run-up to Nationals.

Nico's team all pack into a train, and an hour and a half later they all spill out of it, spirits high and voices chattering. Danny's in a room with Nolan and Noah; he doesn't know Nolan all that well, but the man is kind, and they get on well enough that Danny doesn't really mind sharing.

He lands the toe loop three times in practice. He can hear the Nico that lives in his head telling him not to wear himself out, so he calls it there, skating back over to where his real coach is watching. "Looking good," Nico says.

"I feel good," Danny admits. "Confident."

"Good!" Nico booms. "You should be."

Danny sneaks away long enough to watch Noah and Noemi's compulsory dance, one of three ice dancing events, where they win a small gold by over four points, before Nico finds him and drags him back. In turn, he sees the pair of them in the crowd for his own short program. He spares them a wave before turning back to Nico, who doesn't say anything, just gives him a hug and sends him out.

He lands the quad, thank God, and the rest of his program is as clean and tight as he's ever skated it—60.96, a personal best by quite a few points. Nowhere close to Valentin Wolf's whopping 73.84, of course, but it's enough to scrape him into third place going into the free skate in a few days.

His rinkmates do well too, Mira and Malea making up two-thirds of the ladies' podium, and the Rohner siblings pulling a silver overall. Noah and Noemi take the ice dance gold after their original and free dances, and Danny jumps on Noemi as soon as they're clear of the podium. She squeezes him back and passes him off to Noah, who claps him in a one-armed hug without hesitation. He smells like sweat and cologne. "Now your turn," he says, laughing. "Go knock them dead."

"I'm not going to beat Valentin," Danny says reasonably.

"Not with that attitude," Noemi says, and he laughs.

From there, Nico bundles him into his free skate costume and warms him up, and then, before Danny can really process what's happened, he's landed his two quads in the free skate and they're wrapping a silver medal around his neck. Even more thrillingly, Valentin Wolf, the Hero of Switzerland, turns to him on the podium and says, "I knew you'd be the one next to me this year."

"What?" Danny says stupidly, gazing up at him.

"I have a nose for it," Valentin says, tapping the organ in question and winking one of his dazzling green eyes with a grin. Danny can't speak, so he just grins back, trying not to look like a dope in front of the cameras.

His parents hang his silver medal up with all his Juniors ones, and Danny goes a little light-headed when he looks at them all.

Unfortunately, Nationals being over means it's suddenly mid-December, and the thing Danny has been dreading is just around the corner. He and Ella schedule a going-away party for Simon three days after classes end, and he and Simon make their proper goodbyes the day after, locking themselves in Danny's room with what's left of his box of condoms.

Danny gets Simon off once with his hands and once with his mouth, staying stretched out on top of him afterward, Simon kissing him lazily. "You're getting so good at that," his best friend-turned-temporary-boyfriend says tiredly, running a hand down Danny's back.

Danny preens. "Practice makes perfect, I guess." He kisses Simon again. "Was there anything you wanted to try before you go, that we haven't already done?"

"Mmm, there was one thing I read about." Simon pushes a curl of hair out of Danny's eyes. "Do you have any dental dams?"

"No," Danny says. "Wait! Yes." He rolls off of Simon and scrambles for his skate bag, finding the now-dusty box Nico had given him last month shoved in the bottom.

"Do I want to know why they're in your skate bag?" Simon asks.

"It was tremendously awkward, so no," Danny says. He rips it open, pulls one out, and tosses it to Simon. "How do you want me?"

"Face down, trousers off, legs apart," Simon instructs, and Danny hastens to obey, Simon settling himself between Danny's spread thighs.

Danny hears a crinkling of plastic and feels the dam pressed against his hole, making him squirm, and then Simon must lean in because *oh. Oh, Christ.* "*This* is what we use them for?" Danny gasps, exerting all his will not to buck his ass back into Simon's nose. "Oh God, *Simon*, that feels so good." Simon hums against him and licks again, his fingers digging deep into the meat of Danny's ass cheeks, and Danny has to bury his face in a pillow to stifle his moans.

Danny makes Simon swill some of Danny's mouthwash

after and then pins him to the bed, kissing him for twenty minutes before caving to the inevitable and letting him up to dress. "I'll miss you," Simon says, sitting on the edge of the bed where he'd insisted Danny stay, naked and disheveled, to watch him go. "These past four months have been amazing."

Danny reaches out and touches his face. "I'll miss you too," he says honestly. "But you'll keep in touch, and maybe we can visit."

"There's always phone sex if we get lonely," Simon says, and snickers when Danny does. He kisses him one last time and then he's gone, Danny's first love affair packed away as neatly as all the books that had once been on Simon's shelves and are now stowed in boxes in his family's moving truck. Danny sheds a few tears, and then reminds himself that Simon wouldn't want him to cry, and gets up to clean himself off without his parents noticing.

Chapter 5

DANNY'S PHONE BUZZES with incoming texts, around the time some of his rinkmates should be landing at the European Championships.

Noemi: Hey

Noemi: We wanted you to hear this from us first

Noemi: We would have told you at our last practice, but there wasn't a chance

Danny: I'm nervous

Danny: Spit it out

Noah: We're switching coaches next season

Noah: To Coach Meyer

Noah: He's more experienced with ice dance teams than Nico is

Danny: Does Nico know?

Noah: Of course

Noah: He understands

Noah: The press release goes out tomorrow so we wanted to tell you tonight

Danny: :""""""""(

Danny: I'll miss you guys

Danny: The rink won't be the same without you

Noemi: We'll still see each other all the time!!!!!!

Noemi: At competitions and stuff

Noemi: Plus we'll just like hang out

Noemi: I'll make Noah come

Noah: You won't have to make me, Noemi

Danny: *blush*

Danny: Devastated for me, but happy for you guys

Danny: You're gonna crush it

Noah: We knew you'd understand

Danny: In happier news

Danny: Did I tell you Valentin Wolf talked to me and told me he knew I'd medal????

Noah: Only a thousand times

Noemi: Did he smell good? I bet he smelled good

Noah: I bet he smelled like hairspray and sweat, like every other skater in the world

Danny: Who pissed in your Cheerios?

Noah: Don't be foul, Daniel

Noemi: Don't worry, I just smacked him in the head for you

Danny: Thank you, Noemi, my only real friend here

Noah: This after I carried you through Biology

Noah: And was planning to continue to do so through the second semester

Danny: I'm sorry, Noah, you're beautiful and you smell like roses and fresh cut grass

Andrei Lebed had scraped his way into a men's singles silver medal at the Grand Prix Final, inching his way over the bronze finisher on the strength of a surprise quad Salchow in the second half of his free program. He does it again at the Euros, earning another shiny silver. Danny tags him in a congratulatory Facebook post, not expecting him to see it, but Andrei likes the post a few hours later. Feeling bold, Danny sends a friend request, which is immediately accepted. Danny goes to sleep that night grinning as though *he'd* won a silver medal.

Andrei misses the podium by a *hair* at Worlds, but Noah and Noemi and Mira all pull their way onto bronze-level podiums, and Nico's rink ends the season with a celebration, carefully-doled-out glasses of champagne in the bleachers area of the rink. It's bittersweet, because Noah and Noemi won't be at next year's, but it's a good time anyway.

It's been apparent for some time—Danny, out of boredom, put his short program costume on again sometime in February and nearly tore the seams—but as the rink settles into the off-season, it can no longer be denied that Danny is going through a *major* growth spurt. Nico's poor contract nutritionist has to work his ass off trying to keep Danny's protein and caloric intake in pace with his muscles bulking out, and he shoots upward too, nearly nine centimeters by the end of the summer. It makes his jumps a little wobbly for a while, but he pushes through, and Nico starts letting him drill the quadruple Salchow at the end of every practice.

At some point in July, sick of the heat and the hair tickling his face when he spins, Danny takes his father's clippers to his head, leaving just a few centimeters of thick brown hair, instead of the long waves he'd been working with before. The severity of the cut makes the lines of his face look sharper, an impression only helped by the loss of his last vestiges of puppy fat in his cheeks. What's more, by August he can feel the first pricklings of stubble coming in across his cheeks and chin. He'll be shaving them off for a while yet, but some permanent facial hair might be in his future.

In short, by the time the Grand Prix announcements for the next season come out, Danny looks *good*, and he knows it, and it feels *amazing*.

Danny had a quick lunch with Noah and Noemi in May, but they aren't able to get together again until the press conference at the start of the season. They've seen and liked his pictures on Facebook, but he gets the sense that his *transformation* is more startling in person, so he anticipates the event with no small amount of excitement. Odds are Noah won't react to him at all, but there's a *chance*, and Danny clings to it like the little gay boy he is.

Danny: Are you here yet?

Noemi: Pulling into the parking lot now

Noemi: Traffic was hell

Noemi: Plus Meyer can't drive

Noah: Be nice

Noemi: Why? Are you gonna leak my texts to our coach?

Danny: Stop bickering and hurry uuuuuuuup

Danny: I haven't seen you in *ages*

Noah: We're almost there

Noah: Entering the building now

Danny keeps his eye on the door, and he sees his friends enter a few minutes later, making their way through the press chairs to get to the stage. He stands, and laughs when Noah's eyes skitter over him, only to widen and turn back. Danny grins and winks as Noah gives him a full once-over, eyes raking from head to toe. Is that a blush on Noah's cheeks as he nudges Noemi and points? The lights in Danny's eyes means he can't be sure, but he can hope.

"Holy *hell*," Noemi breathes, rushing up the stairs and throwing herself at him. He's taller than she is now, by a good bit, and she squeezes him tightly and steps back. "*Look* at you."

"Hi," he says, grinning down at her.

"You look *amazing*," she tells him, beaming. "Doesn't he, Noah?"

"Yeah," Noah says. It sounds like his mouth is dry. "You—you look great."

"Thanks." Danny winks at him again. Noah coughs and rubs the back of his neck. "I think it's starting soon," Danny says, taking pity on him. "Sit with me?"

They settle into chairs, Danny and Noemi chattering away. Noah is even quieter than usual, Danny notices. It makes him want to grin triumphantly, but he keeps it in, focusing instead on Noemi's story about the new makeup line she'd found for Black people.

The press conference goes about the same as it had the year before. Noah and Noemi announce their season theme as *longing*, which makes Danny squirm a little in his chair. Nine centimeters of growth or not, Noah is still a smidge taller than he is, he can't help but notice.

When it finally gets to his turn, Danny declares his theme this season to be *growth*, which gets him a few titters from the crowd. When he turns back to his seat, Noemi rolls her eyes at him, grinning. "When did you get so charming?" she murmurs to him as he sits back down.

"I've always been charming," he corrects her. "The word you're looking for is *roguish*."

"My mistake," she says drily. He nudges her with his shoulder. She nudges back. Noah reaches across them both, putting his hand on Danny's knee to settle them. Danny swallows heavily. Noemi nudges him again.

Nico tracks him down after the press conference is done, nodding politely to Noah and Noemi. "Ready to go?" he asks Danny.

Danny hugs Noemi again. "Let's not go this long without seeing each other again, okay?" he says.

"No way," she agrees. "Fingers crossed we'll be at some Grand Prix events together."

"If not, at least the Final," Danny declares. He's been scheduled for two events, the Cup of China and the NHK Trophy, so the Final is, for the first time, a possibility. She nods decisively.

Noah holds out his hand. Danny isn't sure they've ever shaken hands before, not even when they met, but he's willing to go with it. Noah's hand is big and dry, and he has a nice, firm grip. "Good luck this season," Noah says. It looks like he's looking at Danny's nose instead of his eyes as he says it.

"You too," Danny says, before letting Nico sweep him away.

"Lots of attention on you this year," Nico comments in the car, Danny buckled into the passenger seat and flipping through Nico's CD collection idly.

He smiles at his coach. "All good." The press hall had gone up in whispers as soon as he'd walked in, titters and gossip about his physical transformation that had made him stand a little taller and straighter and take an extra second unzipping his jacket, for the show of it.

"Mmm," Nico says, eyes on the road. "Let's hope it stays that way."

Danny's two events are in early November and late November, respectively. "Quick turnaround," his mother comments, looking at the schedule.

"I'll have to talk to my teachers about schoolwork," Danny says. "Won't be fun."

His father kisses him on the head. "You'll manage," he says. "You'll be—"

"Magnificent," Danny says with him, grinning.

He scans the skater lists for Noah and Noemi's names. They're scheduled for the Bompard and Skate Canada; no overlap with him. What he *does* notice is Andrei Lebed's name, set down for the Cup of China and the NHK Trophy, same as

Danny. He pulls up his laptop and opens the long-dormant Facebook message window.

Danny: Looks like we'll be seeing a lot of each other this year

Andrei: Good. I've been waiting for you to catch up

Danny: Flattery! Be still my heart

Danny: I didn't keep you waiting long

Andrei: Long enough

Andrei: Growth, huh?

Danny: You watched my press conference?

Andrei: Keeping an eye on the competition

Danny: What's yours this year? I haven't had a chance to look

Andrei: "Ambiguity"

Danny: Well that's…something

Andrei: My coach's idea, not mine

Andrei: My intentions have always been crystal clear

Andrei: See you in Beijing

Danny: Looking forward to it

School isn't the same without Simon. Last semester wasn't either, but it's particularly striking this year, going to the pre-school party with just Ella on his arm. Danny sends him pictures of his newly-defined abs and gets tons of drooling emojis in return, but it's not the same as having Simon actually with him, under him, winking conspiratorially at him.

Danny's teachers this year have heard of him, at least, and most seem willing to work with him around his competition schedule. Only his new physics teacher gives him pushback, but he manages to get enough assignments moved early or late that he thinks he can manage a science workload around competing.

He and Nico commissioned his costumes in August, just before the press conference, and come mid-September they're ready for final approval. His short program one is pretty standard, a white shirt and black slacks tailored narrowly over his ass and legs, a slim black tie to finish it off. His program is set to a slow jazz number and he'd fought hard for a hat, but Nico had overruled him, claiming it would just be distracting.

His free skate, though, is a different beast entirely, with a costume to match. In July, Nico had given in to the inevitable, and Danny's free skate music is a low, sultry, bassy piece that he'd found in a number of club playlists at the end of the school year. His costume is a tight red bodysuit with rhinestones, and he'd spent the summer at Ella's makeup table, learning how to use everything he needs for his face. Makeup is standard for all skaters, the bright lights of the rink being what they are, but this goes beyond the basic foundation and blush he's used to.

Danny: [img]

Danny: [img]

Danny: Short and free respectively

Noemi: Omg!!!!!

Noemi: Smokin

Noemi: Much sexier than anything I ever get to wear

Danny: That's not true

Danny: I saw your blue dress from last year

Danny: Fire

Noemi: Okay, fair

Noemi: That blue did look great on me

Noemi: But this year is dire

Noemi: Our theme is 'longing' so Meyer wants us conservative and repressed

Noemi: Poor Noah looks like he belongs in a marching band

Danny: Omg

Danny: NGL I'd pay a little to see that

Noemi: You won't have to

Noemi: We'll all be at the Final together, right?

Danny: Right!

Danny: I hope so, anyway

Danny: I'm in both my events with Andrei Lebed

Noemi: The men's singles wunderkind?

Noemi: Are you nervous?

Danny: A little

Danny: We've talked a bit and he seems to be expecting a lot from me

Noemi: You'll deliver, babe

Noemi: You always do

Danny: <3 <3 <3

Danny: So will you

Noemi: <3 <3 <3

Noemi: Gotta run, I'm texting while practicing again

Danny: Kill those twizzles!

Danny's life becomes an endless cycle of practice and schoolwork and working out and baked chicken breasts and protein smoothies, over and over and over until suddenly it's November and he has to get on a plane in a few days. He gets the okay to focus on skating from ninety percent of his teachers, packs his goddamned physics textbook into his checked luggage, and runs through his programs one more time for Nico. He has five contingency plans for missed jumps over both programs; he and Nico go over them so often he's saying them in his sleep.

As usual, his parents see him into Nico's car, his father ruffling his hair and telling him to be magnificent. He slings his luggage into the trunk and gets into the passenger seat, and the nerves hit all at once.

"Are you ready, lad?" Nico asks as they pull away from the house.

"You tell me," Danny says, trying not to worry at his fingernail with his teeth.

"I think you are," Nico says, gratifyingly. "But only you know for sure."

Danny groans and buries his face in his hands. "I've never been this nervous before."

"It's your first full season," Nico says. "It's natural." He puts a hand on the back of Danny's neck, wonderfully warm and steadying. "Take it from an old man who's been through this countless times. You'll be fine. Even if you miss the Final, there's always another season."

"I'm not going to miss the Final," Danny says, trying to say it firmly enough that he believes it. "I'm going to make it."

"That's the ticket," Nico says approvingly, and they drive on.

Chapter 6

THE HOTEL IN China is relatively nice, as far as skating hotels go, but it's the shower that really wins Danny over, the powerful water pressure pounding into his neck and back as he conditions his hair after the long, long, cramped flights. Nico had made Danny choose between first class seats or his own room, their budget being what it was, and he'd chosen the room. He'll have to garner enough sponsors this season to ensure both.

He meets Nico outside their rooms and they head out together to find something to eat. Both of them are starving enough that they settle for the first place they find, hot pot on the corner of the block, and they dig in ravenously.

Once they're sated, they wander slowly back to the hotel. It's chilly enough that just this short walk makes Danny wish he'd brought a scarf. As they near the hotel again, a cab pulls up in front of it, discharging two figures that Danny recognizes with a start. That head of shiny blond hair is unmistakable, even in the dark.

Andrei and his coach, a notoriously grumpy raincloud of a man named Fyodor Yolkin, seem to be arguing about something as Danny and Nico draw near. The Swiss men pass under a streetlamp and Andrei notices them, his angry Russian tirade drawing to a close as he takes them in. Yolkin keeps walking, but Andrei stops, eyes sweeping Danny up and down. To Danny's surprise, there's an assessing look in the Yellow Swan's eyes, and a pleased curl to his mouth that Danny thinks he understands, before Andrei nods at them and follows after his coach.

Well. *That's* an interesting development.

Danny quickly looks at Nico to see if he'd noticed, but the

man is studying the wall of the hotel. "Interesting architecture," Danny says, and Nico nods, turning back to him with a smile.

The next day is for practice, getting used to the competition rink and stretching out after their flights. Danny lands all his jumps and flies through his spins and steps until Nico sends him back to the hotel to rest and catch up on his schoolwork. As he's leaving the ice, he sees Andrei step onto it, all coiled power and fierce concentration. He catches sight of Danny looking and winks; Danny bites his lip, a delightful tingling in his nerves, and goes to obey his coach's orders.

Danny wakes the next day like someone has thrown water in his face, all at once with a start. Nico feeds him a carefully nutritious breakfast and sends him for a short run to get out his nerves, and then they head over to the rink.

The morning passes quickly, lunch a protein shake and a granola bar. Danny is in the second group to skate, and spends the time warming up slowly and steadily, Nico occasionally correcting his form with a hand on his arm or his back.

When he takes the ice for his short program, he's surprised to find himself calm. Nico doesn't say anything, and Danny doesn't need him to; they hug, and he heads out in a contemplative silence.

It's a good skate. It's not the best skate of the day, not by a long shot, but when the announcer reads out his score and Nico squeezes his shoulders, Danny feels nothing but contentment with the day's work. The congratulatory message in his Facebook from Andrei doesn't hurt either.

There are two days between men's singles events, and Danny spends them constantly turning his head, catching flashes of yellow out of the corners of his eye that vanish whenever he tries to look more closely. Eventually he stops chasing them; if Andrei wants to flit around him like a moth around a candle, Danny isn't going to complain.

Danny's in fifth going into the free skate, and Andrei is in third. Danny knows his chances of making the podium are low;

he only has two quads in his free skate, one toe loop and one Salchow, fewer than Andrei's and others' three. But the chance is there, and he's going to try for it. *Hey, Andrei*, he thinks to himself as he takes center ice, falling into his starting pose. *Watch this.*

It isn't, in the end, enough to podium, and there's the bitter sting of disappointment that goes along with a close fourth place. It is, however, enough to earn him a body coming up behind him at the banquet the next night, and a familiar voice saying in surprising, accented German, "You did well."

Danny turns to see Andrei lounging against the wall next to him, a glass of champagne in hand as he surveys the rest of the party. "Congratulations on your silver," he says, also in German.

"It'll be gold next time," Andrei says carelessly. His eyes flick over to Danny's face. "And you'll be next to me."

"Fingers crossed," Danny says.

Andrei waves this aside. His trademark hair is up in a half-ponytail, tendrils falling to frame his face; he looks sharp, elegant, almost dangerous, even in the slightly stodgy suit he's chosen for the evening. "I'm pleased you're finally properly competitive," he says, taking a sip from his drink.

"Why?" Danny asks, honestly curious. "I'm flattered you've taken an interest in me, but why me?"

Andrei shrugs. "A man needs a foil."

Danny snorts, taken aback. "I'm your foil now?"

"I don't mean it as an insult," Andrei says, looking more sharply at him. "Our styles are very different, yet your scores are roughly where mine were at that level, and both are high. You won Juniors the year after me, and we have very different public images. To be each other's foil seems natural to me."

"Hmm." Danny eyes him, looking for mockery, but gets nothing but sharp-edged sincerity. He shrugs. "Alright. Sure. I'll be your foil. Or maybe you'll be mine."

Andrei grins, honed and glinting like a knife. "I'll be the one in gold, Daniel Schaer."

"We'll see about that," Danny says, returning the grin. Adrenaline is racing through his veins. He holds out his own glass and Andrei toasts him. "See you in Tokyo," Danny says after they've both drunk, taking a step away. "Hopefully in a better suit. That one doesn't flatter you at all." He turns, hearing Andrei's shocked laughter behind him, and goes to find Nico.

The rest of November doesn't seem nearly long enough to have two events before the NHK Trophy at the end; Danny barely has time to churn out three essays and watch Noah and Noemi earn silver medals in Paris before Nico is packing him into another set of international flights, this time to Japan. "This is the life of a competitive skater, Danny," Nico says, watching him groan and crack his neck when they pull into the gate in Tokyo. "You'll have to get used to it."

"I'd get used to it easier in first class," Danny grumbles.

This competition has a much tighter turnaround than the Cup of China, packing all its events into three days. They land at dawn on Thursday, leaving them enough time for a shower and a few hours' sleep before afternoon practice. Andrei is there, looking just as tired as Danny feels, and they nod at each other across the ice.

The next day holds the short programs. Danny has spent the last three weeks refining his after the Cup of China, tweaking his Grades of Execution and running contingency after contingency. He must be visibly fretting by the time the pairs podium clear off the ice, turning it over to men's singles, because Nico says, "There's a whole different crop of skaters at this one, Danny. You have a good chance of medaling here and making the Final." Danny needs a silver medal or above to garner enough points to make the Final; technically possible, but daunting.

"I know," Danny says. "I *know*, I do. But."

"But," Nico says kindly, putting his hand on Danny's shoulder. "You'll be fine."

"I wish you'd let me add another quad to my free skate."

"We'll do it for the Final," Nico tells him. "You don't need it here."

His short program goes as well as can be hoped for. It's a personal best; he finishes out the day in a solid third place, behind Andrei and a skater from Canada. Andrei finds him before he leaves the rink to put a thrilling hand on the back of Danny's neck and say, "Stay focused. I told you, I want you up there next to me."

"I will," Danny promises. It comes out more earnest than he intends, but Andrei just nods seriously and releases him, his hand sliding down Danny's neck and across his shoulder as he removes it. Danny tingles again at the glint in Andrei's eyes.

Their day off passes in a blink, and then it's time to take the ice again. "You're *sure* I shouldn't add a surprise quad in?" Danny asks Nico for the dozenth time as he warms up.

"Not without practicing first," Nico says sharply. "Promise me, Danny."

"I promise," Danny says reluctantly.

In the end, Nico's right, and so is Andrei; he doesn't need the extra quad. His programs as they are, plus a nasty fall from the skater after him, garner him a silver medal and a place at Andrei's right hand on the podium. "Told you," Andrei calls down to him from the top step. Danny just looks back up at him, letting a little bit of the excited heat he feels into his eyes. Andrei's own eyes narrow, the corner of his mouth turning up.

The hotel is within walking distance of the rink. Danny can feel Andrei a few hundred feet behind him and Nico as they approach it. "You go ahead," he tells Nico. "I want a few more minutes in the fresh air." Nico leaves him, and Danny leans against the hotel's outer wall, watching as Andrei approaches. The other skater has shaken his coach too, and he lifts an eyebrow as he draws within range of the hotel. Danny steps out and together they walk inside.

"I don't have your number," Andrei says in the elevator. "Give me your phone." Danny does, and watches Andrei enter himself in and send himself a text. "There," he says, passing it back to Danny. "No more Facebook."

"No more Facebook," Danny agrees, leading him out of the elevator and to the door of his room.

The atmosphere, tense as it was in the elevator, only sharpens once they're inside Danny's room with the door closed. "Take off your shoes," Danny says, toeing his own off. "Stay awhile."

Andrei grins sidelong at him and slips out of his shoes, unzipping his jacket as well and tossing it aside. To Danny's secret delight, he also reaches up to the tie in his hair and works it loose, his shoulder-length hair falling from its ponytail to settle around his neck. "You're really beautiful," Danny hears himself say quietly. Andrei flushes a pretty red, taking a step closer.

Danny takes a step closer too, and then they both take another, until they're nose to nose. Andrei's eyes are wide and his breath is coming in fast and sharp, so it falls to Danny to reach up and put a hand on the side of his neck. He looks at Andrei, a question in his eyes, and waits for Andrei's nod before leaning in and gently touching their mouths together.

Andrei responds instantly, his lips slotting together with Danny's and his hands coming up to curl in the fabric of Danny's jacket. "Take this off," he murmurs against Danny's lips, tugging at it. Danny laughs and shrugs out of it, and then he takes Andrei's hand and leads him to the bed.

They end up stretched out against the pillows, Danny's torso pinning Andrei down. Andrei gets a hand in his hair and kisses him hard, his tongue working between Danny's lips to brush against Danny's as he lets out a relieved little groan. He puts his other hand on Danny's neck, a hot pressure that makes Danny grin against his lips and press closer.

He lets Andrei set the pace, his only venture to slip three fingers beneath the fabric of Andrei's shirt to touch his skin. Andrei hisses into his mouth, almost a moan, and Danny doesn't push, just uses them to caress a few inches of Andrei's waist as they kiss and kiss and kiss.

Andrei grows bolder, pushing up against him with his chest

and cocking a leg to wrap around Danny's where they're tangled on the comforter. His fingers tug at Danny's hair, and then again at the noise that elicits. He smells like hairspray and something foresty, and he tastes like raspberry Chapstick.

Danny breaks away from his mouth to press a kiss to the corner of his lips, then the jut of his jaw, then just under his ear.

"Don't—" Andrei starts as Danny moves down his neck.

"I know," Danny murmurs. He keeps his kisses light, no suction to avoid a mark, trailing them down one side of Andrei's tense throat and up the middle, until he kisses Andrei's chin and takes his mouth again. They're both breathing heavily, letting out soft little sounds of pleasure that go straight to Danny's cock.

There comes a natural stopping point, an end to their momentum as they breath against each other's lips. "I should go," Andrei murmurs regretfully. "Early flight tomorrow."

"Me too," Danny says. He steals another kiss before leaning back, letting Andrei sit up and adjust the hem of his shirt. Andrei's ears are red, he notices with delight, and reaches out to touch one. Andrei looks at him curiously as he reaches for his shoes. "Like I said," Danny says. "You're really beautiful."

Andrei pulls his shoes on and stands. He puts one hand on either side of Danny's face and leans down to kiss him deeply, tongue stealing in for one last taste before he goes. "Thank you," he murmurs. "For the compliment and the evening."

"Both were my pleasure," Danny says. "You can have a repeat of either anytime."

Andrei laughs, low and a little dangerous-sounding. "I'll take you up on that." He picks his jacket up off the floor and slings it over his shoulder. "See you at the Final," he says, and then he's gone.

As soon as the door clicks shut behind him, Danny falls back onto the bed, fingers scrabbling at the waistband of his trousers. He licks across his palm and wraps it around his cock, letting out a moan as he strokes himself. It's over in a heartbeat, leaving him panting and loose, laughing as he catches his breath.

Chapter 7

BEFORE THE GRAND Prix Finals comes Nationals. The train to La Chaux-de-Fonds is only an hour and fifteen minutes. As has become tradition, although thankfully not for much longer, Danny spends it frantically doing homework, writing out his physics lab methodology on top of his textbook while his rinkmates either chatter away or, for the younger ones, do the same. The hotel is within walking distance of the train station, so they all load themselves down with luggage and make the trek. Danny is bunking alone this year, which is a relief; honestly, he thinks his days of roommates at competitions are behind him.

He catches sight of Noemi in the hotel lobby and sneaks up behind her, wrapping his hands around her eyes. She jabs back with her elbow and laughs. "No one else uses that cologne," she says. "I could smell you a mile away."

"Lies," Danny declares, mock-offended. "I smell like train, and I've a moderate hand with the cologne."

"Whatever you say, love," she says, patting him on the cheek. "Noah's around here somewhere; want to grab dinner tonight?"

"Sure," Danny says. "Let me drop my bags in my room and wash my face and I'll meet you." He kisses her on the cheek and makes for the desk to check in.

Clothes shaken out, excess cologne discreetly washed off, and face crisp and clean, he texts Noemi and gets an address three blocks away for what appears on his Maps app to be a Thai place. She and Noah are already seated when he arrives, but Noah stands as he approaches.

"Good to see you," Noah says, holding out his hand. Danny shakes it, amused, and sits across from them, flipping the menu open.

"Congratulations on making the Final," he tells them, scanning for an appropriate food option with a competition the next day. "You too," they say in unison. Noemi lays a hand on his arm. When he looks up, she's smiling at him, and there's a pleased quirk to the edge of Noah's mouth that means he's as happy as Danny is that they'll all be there together.

They order, the waiter taking their menus away, and Noemi leans forward across the table. "To the meat of the matter," she says, ducking her head close to Danny's. "How nervous are you, with Valentin out of the game?"

Danny groans theatrically and she cackles. "Don't remind me," he says. "Ever since he announced he was sitting this season out, God knows Nico won't shut up about *this is your year, Danny*. I'm losing my *mind*."

"No need to lose your mind," Noah says. Danny looks at him. "The gold is all but yours," he goes on, leaning back in his chair. The top few buttons of his shirt are undone, revealing a very distracting strip of collarbone.

"All but," Danny says, forcing his eyes back up to Noah's face. There's a little twinkle in Noah's eye that Danny immediately decides not to read into. "With Valentin gone, it's anyone's game."

"Nonsense," Noemi says. "You're the best men's skater Switzerland has, without him."

"I doubt he's gone for good, anyway," Danny says. "He'll be back for the next Olympics."

"All the same," Noah says. "It's yours in the meantime. There's no one else in your league."

Danny can feel himself start to glow under Noah's praise, and to offset it, he shoots back, "And what about you two? Is anyone else even competing in ice dance, or can you just waltz in and take the medal?"

"First of all, we won't be waltzing," Noemi says. "The compulsory is the paso doble."

"Sexy," Danny drawls.

"And yes, there are other competitors."

"You'll sweep the floor with them," he declares. She dimples at him, and when he looks at Noah, the man is smiling confidently, still lounging back in his chair.

Their food comes then, and conversation slows as they eat. It's decent fare, filling and well-made, and when the check comes, Noah snatches it before either Danny or Noemi can move.

"Hey," Noemi objects, grabbing for it as he holds it out of her reach.

"We'll split it like always," Danny says. "What's the total, Noah?"

Noah shakes his head, slipping his card into the check sleeve and shutting it tightly. "Nope. It's on me tonight."

"On our sponsors, you mean," Noemi says, relenting. "Fine. If you want to play the gentleman, I won't complain."

"Danny?" Noah asks, his eyes focusing on Danny's face. "Any complaints from you?"

There's something going on here that Danny doesn't quite understand, an undercurrent he's *almost* tapped into, but he just shrugs. "And they say chivalry is dead."

Noah's eyes grow sharp, until Danny almost has to shift under his gaze, and then he backs down and lays the check sleeve on the table with a nod, his card sticking out of the edge.

Nationals is another quick turnaround, three days to pack everything in. With men's gold on the line, Danny is busy and stressed, but he takes the time to go see Noah and Noemi perform. Noah does look a bit like he belongs in a marching band during their original dance, it's true, but their dances are pitch-perfect all the same, so full of longing and repressed desire that Danny is almost moved to tears. It's a well-earned gold wrapped around each of their necks, and Danny shoots them both congratulatory texts before Nico drags him back to practice.

His short program goes well, leaving him in first place

going into the free by a solid four points. As he straps himself into the bodysuit for his final skate, he focuses on steady breathing and clear thoughts. *Just because Valentin isn't here, it doesn't mean the gold is mine just because I'm in first place so far,* he tells himself a million times. *I have to work for it.* Noe Ott, currently in second, has just as much chance as Danny does to take the title.

"Focus," Nico tells him. "This will determine Euros and Worlds. You're guaranteed spots in both, unless you mess this free skate up. So don't mess it up."

"Reassuring," Danny says drily.

"I wouldn't be honest if I didn't think you could handle it," Nico counters. "Keep your head and you'll be fine."

Danny sees Noah and Noemi in the crowd as he takes center stage, both of them holding either side of a sign with his name on it. He snorts to himself, takes his pose, and waits for the music.

As he skates, he keeps thinking of that sign, held by his friends. He thinks of the collarbone Noah had on display last night, he thinks of the way Noah's hand went to his lower back as he escorted him out of the restaurant, he thinks of the way Andrei's hair felt between his fingers as Danny kissed him senseless. He lands both his quads and earns himself a national title.

It's his first time at the top of a podium since Juniors, and it feels *good.* The cameras flash in his eyes; the gold of the medal clashes *horribly* with his bright red costume; someone at some point has given him flowers to hold, and their scent is all that's keeping him tethered as the elation has its way with him.

"Good job," Nico tells him on the train back to Bern. "Do it again in Goyang."

Danny spends the next four days frantically training his free skate with three quads, and then they're off again, a twenty-hour flight to South Korea that Danny spends half asleep and half working on *fucking* physics homework. Nico wakes him when they land, and Danny is asleep within half an hour of arriving at the hotel, just long enough to strip off his clothes and wash the plane from his hair.

He wakes to find a text from Andrei.

Andrei: Just arrived. Let's have dinner.

Danny: Not up for anything more complex than room service, I'm afraid

Andrei: I'm in, if you don't mind company. Bill my food to my room.

Danny: Come on up, then

Andrei sends him his order and Danny calls it down, stretching the residual soreness out of his body as he does. Andrei arrives before the food does, slipping past Danny into the room with a trail of the same foresty scent he'd had before. "How were your flights?" he asks, settling onto Danny's bed like he owns it and kicking his shoes off.

"Hellish," Danny says, going to sit next to him. "Yours?"

"Disgusting." Andrei frowns at the memory, and Danny can't help but lean in and catch that pout with his own lips.

Andrei responds with a delighted little purr in the back of his throat, reaching up to twist a hand into Danny's collar and pull him closer. They make out for the twenty minutes it takes for the food to arrive, and Danny flushes with pride at the bitten pinkness of Andrei's lips as they set into their meals.

"Congratulations on your Nationals medal," Andrei says over his steak. "Even without Wolf, your performance was impressive."

"Thanks?" Danny says, trying to work out if he's been insulted. "Are you nervous for yours?"

"No," Andrei says firmly, shaking his head. "I don't get nervous; I get focused."

"Must be nice."

"Are you nervous now?" Andrei asks curiously, regarding him.

"Sure." Danny shrugs. "I'm still a relative newcomer, all things considered. My medaling would be an upset."

"So upset them," Andrei says, taking another bite. "It's as simple as that."

"I admire your outlook on the world," Danny says drily, turning back to his own chicken. They finish their food and push the plates aside, flopping down on the bed to face each other on their sides. "Have you added a third quad to your free skate?" Andrei asks, his nose almost brushing Danny's.

Danny nods. "Not sure how it'll go, but I'm going to try."

"Good," Andrei says. "I respect trying."

Danny props himself up on one elbow. "Well, I'm glad you respect me."

"Of course I do," Andrei says. He reaches up to trail one finger along Danny's jaw. He needs to shave; Andrei's finger scrapes against stubble, and it makes him shiver. "I wouldn't be attracted to you if I didn't respect you."

That's all it takes, that and the pull of Andrei's hand on his jaw; Danny dives into Andrei's mouth, which opens for him with a soulful groan. He braces his forearm against the mattress and puts the other hand on Andrei's waist, pulling their bodies tight together as Andrei takes his tongue.

Andrei's leg hitches up around his waist, pulling their hips against each other, and Danny moans. Andrei bites his lips and pulls at his hair, and Danny gives as good as he gets, until they're both rumpled and groaning into each other's mouths.

They kiss and grind against each other until the sounds of their hook-up are cut through by a text alert Danny doesn't recognize. Andrei groans, this time in frustration, and fishes his phone out of his pocket. "It's Fyodor," he says with a grimace, tapping at the screen. "He wants to see me."

Danny sighs and rolls off him. Andrei sits up and winces. "I can't see him in this condition," he says, looking down at his lap, where there is a definite bulge in his sweatpants. "He'll kill me."

Danny puts a hand on his knee. "Want some help with it?"

Andrei looks up at him, eyes a bright, sparkling gray. "Would you?" Danny nods and Andrei bites his lip. "Alright," he breathes.

"Sweatpants down," Danny says. Andrei stands long enough to shimmy them to mid-thigh, revealing a cock that's as sturdy and graceful as he is, and then sits down again. Danny licks across his palm, then catches Andrei's eye. "Hey," he says. "Kiss me." Andrei obeys instantly, and as his lips interlock with Danny's, Danny wraps his spit-slick hand around Andrei's cock.

Andrei groans, deep and loud, and grabs at him as he starts to stroke, slow at first and picking up the pace as he goes. Andrei loses the ability to kiss back fairly quickly, so Danny nudges his head aside and goes for his throat, leaving light, barely-there kisses as his hand works him fast and tight.

"Yes," Andrei whines, tossing his head back even further. "Yes, Danny, that's so good. Feels so good, your hand..." He trails off into what must be Russian, and then he rocks his head forward again, pressing his cheek to Danny's as his cock pulses in Danny's hand and erupts.

Danny kisses him through the comedown, hand still moving slowly on his cock until he can breathe steadily again. "Thank you," Andrei murmurs, tilting up to brush his lips over Danny's one more time.

Before he can do much more, his phone chimes again and he scowls. "I really have to go," he says, flicking his eyes down at Danny's crotch, with a noticeable bulge of its own.

"Go," Danny says. "I'll get off in the shower thinking of you."

"I'll pay you back," Andrei says, standing and pulling his sweatpants up. "Soon."

"No rush," Danny says, leaning back on his hands as Andrei pulls his shoes on. "We have days."

Andrei grabs him for a final, hard kiss. "Soon," he promises, looking Danny in the eye, and then departs, leaving Danny to another long, hot shower and the tightness of his own hand.

Chapter 8

DANNY WAKES THE day after the short programs later than usual, although his skater's discipline ensures it isn't *too* late. Still plenty of time before morning practice, at least, and plenty of time to deal with the situation in his briefs that dreaming of Andrei brought on. Before tending to it, though, he checks his phone.

Andrei: I bought condoms.

Danny: You didn't have to. I have plenty

Andrei: Good for me to have my own. I thought I might catch you with a morning erection you needed help with.

Danny: [img]

Andrei: I'll be right up

Danny doesn't bother dressing, and Andrei gives him an appreciative look up and down when he arrives. He pushes Danny back to the bed and kisses him, tangling a hand in his hair and tugging a little. "Ready?"

Danny laughs. "Ready." He lifts his hips enough to pull his briefs down and off, tossing them aside.

"You really are quite gorgeous," Andrei says conversationally, sinking to his knees between Danny's legs.

"Thank you," Danny murmurs, running his hand along the top of Andrei's head.

Andrei produces a condom from his pocket and Danny tears it open and rolls it on. As his preliminary move, Andrei reaches out and runs a finger from tip to base, making Danny hiss, and then he grasps hold, tilts Danny's cock toward his mouth, and takes him between his lips.

"Oh Christ," Danny swears, stomach tensing as Andrei starts to work him slowly, a few inches at a time disappearing between his stretched lips. "*Fuck*, who taught you how to suck cock?" Andrei's *good* at it, teasing him, flicking his tongue against the vein, gently stroking what can't fit in his mouth with his hand. Andrei just hums around him and drops him a wink before refocusing.

Danny leans his torso back, bracing himself on his elbows, and Andrei swarms up into his lap, until he's taking Danny into his mouth almost vertically. Danny lets himself groan loudly, balling his fists into the sheets to keep from thrusting up into Andrei's mouth. "Fuck, that's good," he says, and Andrei's hollowed cheeks flush a deeper red. "You're gonna make me come, Andrei, just keep doing that, *oh*."

Andrei works him right up to the brink and over, sucking him hard as the aftershocks pulse through his cock into the condom. "Shit," Danny breathes, hanging his head back. "That was *amazing*."

Andrei leans back, smugness written all across his face. "No point doing something if you're not going to do it well."

"Can I do anything for you?" Danny asks, sitting back up.

Andrei shakes his head. "I'm good, I just wanted to pay you back."

"Andrei," Danny says. "It's not an exchange."

Andrei rolls his eyes. "I *know*, Danny, I just didn't want to say that I dreamed of your cock in my mouth last night. Woke up drooling."

"Now, why wouldn't you want to say that?" Danny asks with a smirk. "Seems a fine thing to say to me."

"Ugh," Andrei says expressively, turning on his heel. "You better not slack off," he calls over his shoulder as he opens the door. "I want a proper fight." Danny salutes him, and he lets the door fall shut behind him.

Danny scrapes a fourth-place finish at the Final after the free skates, and Andrei a silver. They have just enough time to wink at each other before their coaches sweep them back home to their respective countries.

There's a scant few weeks between the Final and the European Championships, and Nico and Danny spend them drilling his free skate with three quads, until he's seeing jump compositions behind his eyes when he sleeps. Then it's off to Helsinki.

They arrive two days before the start of the competition, and to Danny's delight, Noah and Noemi do too. They meet for dinner in a little restaurant three blocks from the competition hotel. "Are you going to do a mating ritual over the check again?" Noemi asks baldly, a glass of wine in. Danny snorts.

"It's not a mating dance," Noah says mildly. "And no, if you're so insistent, you can pay your own way this time."

"It's sponsors!" Noemi says, doing jazz hands. "It's all sponsors!" Noah rolls his eyes but covertly winks at Danny.

"I'm knackered," Noemi says as they walk back to the hotel. It's snowing lightly, a sweet dusting that makes the Finnish street look a bit like a fairy tale. "It's a bath and bed for me."

"I should do the same," Noah says. "What floor are you on, Danny?"

"Twenty-seven," Danny says, fishing his key out of his pocket to read the room number.

"I'm on twenty-six."

"Fifteen for me," Noemi says. "Which means I get my own room *and* my own elevator." They've arrived at the hotel, and duck into the warmth of the lobby gratefully. "Good night, boys," she says, walking toward the elevator that will take her to her floor. "See you at practice tomorrow."

Noah and Danny wander over to the elevators that service floors twenty-five to thirty. "Are you nervous?" Danny asks, falling back on the conversational staple of every competition.

"Not about the competition, no."

"What *are* you nervous about?" Danny asks, but Noah just shakes his head and steps into the newly-arrived elevator.

The elevators in this hotel are slower than any Danny has been in before, and it takes a long time to get to floor twenty-six. He becomes aware of Noah's eyes on him, steady and heavy like a weight, and looks up at him.

Noah's expression is intense, the face Danny has seen on him before every competitive skate since they were rinkmates. As Danny watches, he reaches out, slowly pushing his fingers into Danny's hair. "You have a leaf," he murmurs, pulling it out and flicking it to the floor. A tingle starts at the place Noah had touched and spreads over Danny's whole body, and as Noah takes a step closer and leans in Danny lets his eyes fall shut and—

The elevator pulls to a stop. Danny opens his eyes when he remains unkissed to see that Noah has taken a step back, a look of barely-suppressed fear in his eyes. "I…" he starts, then stops, and tries again. "Good night, Daniel," he says, and then he leaves the elevator, the doors shutting behind him.

"Good night," Danny says to the empty chamber.

He pulls a respectable fifth place at the Euros, and again at Worlds, around training and schoolwork and mutual blowjobs with Andrei and texts with Noemi. Noah spends enough time with them that Danny can't accuse the man of avoiding him, but he resolutely avoids being alone with Danny. Danny takes the sting of hurt and channels it into his skating.

For once, there's something to look forward to even after Worlds is done and dusted. In May, Danny graduates with his matura, and three weeks later moves out of his childhood home into his own place, a tiny studio apartment in the city proper. It's closer to the rink, closer to Noemi, and closer to the gay bars he's looking forward to spending some time in over the off-season. His mother cries when she brings the last box in, and Danny does too, a little, but when they leave and it's just him and his moving-day pizza, he can't deny the rush of joy and relief he feels.

Nico sets him the task of choosing his own music in early June, and Danny runs through every playlist he has before admitting defeat. There's a record store twenty minutes away from his apartment, and one hot day he stops in on his run to peruse their collections, only to find himself perused in turn by the boy behind the counter. The boy is long and lanky, older than Danny but not by much, dressed in a black T-shirt and dramatic eyeliner. Not at all the sort of man Danny minds eyeing him up on his daily run.

Danny catches his eye, expecting the boy to blush or turn away at having been caught, but instead he just grins widely and winks. Danny feels a thrum of excited energy run up his spine, his own lips turning up in a grin just as wide, and makes his way up to the counter.

The boy's name tag says *Laurin*. "Looking for music to skate to?" Laurin drawls, leaning back in his chair as Danny approaches.

"You know who I am?" Danny asks, surprised.

Laurin nods. "I come from a big figure skating household," he says. His eyes travel up and down Danny's body before coming to rest again on his face. "Been following your career quite closely."

Danny lets a little bit more of his smirk out. "Well, you're right. I'm looking for something to skate to next season. What have you got for me?"

"Hmm," Laurin says. He looks over at the clock, then back to Danny. "Nothing today, but we might have something tomorrow. You'd better come back."

Danny laughs. "Had I?" He ogles Laurin in turn, triumph coiling in his stomach when his gaze makes the boy shift in his chair. "Alright," he says. "See you tomorrow, then."

He goes back the next day, in a deep blue tank top that Noemi says brings out his eyes and the shortest shorts he can find in his closet. Laurin lights up when he enters, straightening as he comes through the door. "Wasn't sure you'd be back," Laurin says.

Danny lays his hands wide on the counter, shifting his

weight to loom over it and flex his arms. "You said you'd have something for me," he says, and Laurin grins.

"I do." He picks up a record that's laying on the counter. "Listen to this." He sets it in the player beside him and turns it on.

It's an instrumental piece that Danny has never heard before, all string instruments and tempo. "Is that a harp?" he asks. Laurin nods, a light in his eyes. "I like it," Danny declares when the song is over. "Perfect for my short program. Do you have it in CD form?" Laurin rolls his eyes theatrically but produces a CD and rings Danny up. "Wonderful," Danny says, showing a bit of teeth. "And what about my free?"

Laurin winks at him. "It took me all night to conjure your short program up. You'd better come back tomorrow if you want a long program as well."

Danny does, and goes back the day after that just for the way Laurin brightens when he sees him, and the day after that, and so on for three weeks. He learns that Laurin is twenty and home for university break, that he's a pansexual vegetarian goth, and that he's just as much of a music snob as one would expect of a boy who spends his school vacations working in a record shop. "You really must get a record player," Laurin says to him one day, taking his break with Danny in the alley behind the shop as they share cups of instant coffee from the break room. "It's about the integrity of the music."

"They can't project records onto the rink," Danny says reasonably, "and I'm not buying my music in duplicate." Laurin tuts at him. "Besides," Danny goes on, "what would you have to chide me over if I gave in?"

"I wouldn't have to chide you at all," Laurin says. His eyes, big and brown, go a little molten. "I could spend my time doing all sorts of other things to you."

Danny laughs. "You talk a big game, Laurin, but it's been almost a month and you've yet to make a move."

Laurin blinks, then laughs. "Alright. You've got me there. Cards on the table: I like you." He smiles. "Let's have a fling."

Danny raises an eyebrow. "A fling?"

Laurin nods. "I'm going back to university in the fall, and you'll be busy with skating, so getting serious about each other seems inadvisable. But that doesn't mean we can't mean something to each other in the meantime."

Danny considers this. He's never had a fling before. "Alright," he says after a moment. "Sure. Let's do it."

Laurin grins at him. "I'm going to kiss you now," he warns.

"I've only been waiting," Danny says, and they're both still laughing when Laurin pulls him into the kiss.

They're in Danny's bed two weeks later, music playing low and bassy as they kiss lazily and send their hands up each other's shirts, when Laurin finds out that Danny has never tried anal sex. "Impossible," he declares. "You have too fine an ass never to have had anything in it." He sends his hand from where it's been tweaking Danny's nipple to run over the body part in question, giving it a firm squeeze.

"Fix it, then," Danny murmurs into his neck, sucking hard where it meets his jaw.

"You would want me to?" Laurin asks. Danny scrapes his teeth over the suck mark and Laurin moans low in his throat, tipping his head back.

"Sure," Danny says, lying back on the bed and tugging Laurin on top of him. "I trust you. Why not?"

Laurin's eyes are molten again when Danny looks into them, and the lazy afternoon ends with Laurin's head between Danny's thighs, three of his fingers buried deep in Danny's ass while Danny writhes and moans weakly.

Danny decides on bottoming first, and they pick an evening where he doesn't have to skate the next day. Laurin opens him up, slow and steady like they've been doing for days, until Danny is panting with need, and then Danny settles himself in Laurin's lap and carefully, achingly inches himself down.

"God," Danny gasps when he's fully seated, head thrown back and breath coming in ragged gasps. "*Christ*, Laur, this feels incredible."

"You *look* incredible," Laurin manages. He's propped up against the pillows, feet planted to give Danny something to rock against, and he's running his hands all over Danny's torso and thighs. "You're so beautiful, Danny, do you know that? The most beautiful person I could have imagined to spend my summer with."

Danny laughs, putting a hand on his shoulder and starting to rock back and forth, moaning ecstatically at the way Laurin's cock pulls and catches at his rim. "Fuck me," he whispers, biting his lip. Laurin gets a hand around the back of his neck and pulls him into a kiss, his hips starting to move in tandem with Danny's.

Danny fucks Laurin two days later, Laurin on his hands and knees and slamming back into him with every thrust. They collapse onto each other afterward, panting heavily, and when Laurin catches his breath he props himself up on one elbow and asks, "So which do you prefer?"

"I don't know," Danny says honestly. He pushes a lock of jet-black hair off Laurin's forehead and grins. "We'd better do them both again, just to be sure." Laurin laughs breathlessly and falls on him, mouth-first.

They take their leave of each other in late August, a farewell sixty-nining the night before Laurin's train back to university. Danny comes first, and once he gets his head back on his shoulders he throws his weight over Laurin's hips and sucks him dry, Laurin's fingers petting shakily through his hair.

Laurin kisses his sore mouth afterward. "It's been lovely, my dear," he murmurs. "Thank you for spending your summer with me."

"It was my pleasure." Danny trails a finger down Laurin's cheek. "I'll miss you."

"As I will miss you," Laurin says. "But we'll have the memories." He smirks. "Call me when they make the documentary about you. I'll say nothing but complimentary things."

Danny laughs. "I'll hold you to that." He kisses Laurin's grin one more time, walks him to the door, and watches him go down the stairs with nothing but contentment in his heart.

Chapter 9

DANNY IS SCHEDULED for two events in the next Grand Prix series: the Rostelecom Cup and Skate America. There's no overlap with Noah and Noemi, he notes with disappointment, but Andrei will be in New York with him.

Without schoolwork to keep on top of, he's able to throw himself fully into training in a way he never has before. Nico loves the music Laurin found for him, and his programs are designed to maximize his strengths, personality and triple flips and spins. They take his full focus and energy as the summer ends and the series begins. He's feeling good about them by the time October rolls around, but every time he takes a look at the lineups of the two events, he gets a nervous little quiver in his stomach.

Andrei: Half my rink will be in Moscow with you

Danny: I know, I'm a little terrified

Danny: It'll be hard enough to make the Final this year without all of Fyodor's Finest staring me down

Andrei: You're competitive against every one of us and you know it

Andrei: That's not the point

Danny: What's the point, then?

Andrei: I could convince Fyodor to let me tag along

Andrei: If I wouldn't be a distraction to you

Danny: Omg

Danny: You'd come, seriously?

Andrei: It's been a lonely summer

Andrei: And besides, I wouldn't have to skate

Andrei: Opens up opportunities for certain activities

Danny: Activities?

Andrei: I'm saying you could fuck me, if you wanted to

Danny: Holy shit, Andrei

Danny: What the hell. Yes, please come if you can swing it

Danny: I promise not to let you distract me on the ice

Andrei: I'll hold you to that

Danny is buzzing with anticipation by the time their plane touches down in Moscow. He turns his phone on to find a very lewd picture of Andrei in his hotel room, captioned *Waiting for you*, and has to hide his blush from Nico.

He must not do a very good job, because in the cab to the hotel, Nico leans toward him and says, "I hear Andrei Lebed has tagged along to watch the Cup."

Danny schools his face into what he hopes is a neutral expression and says, "Scoping out the competition, no doubt."

"No doubt," Nico says. They ride in silence for another minute, and then Nico sighs and says, "Please be careful, Danny." Danny looks at him; his face is solemn and caring. "I've seen affairs between rivals go south so many, many times."

Danny swallows hard and shakes his head. "It's not like that with me and Andrei. We're not having an affair. We're just friends who…" He can't bring himself to finish that sentence. "My heart's not in any danger, Nico," he says instead. Despite himself, Noah's face in the elevator last winter flashes across his mind. "I promise I'll be fine."

"Okay, lad," Nico says, patting him on the knee. "I trust you, and it's not my job to judge you. I just worry."

"I appreciate it," Danny says honestly, earning himself a kindly smile from his coach.

Andrei jumps on him as soon as Danny's showered and presented himself at Andrei's room, pinning him to the door by the mouth and hips.

"You did miss me," Danny says, amused, as Andrei breaks away to lick down his neck.

"Fyodor barely let me have an off-season," Andrei growls. "I spent my summer in an ice rink, with no one to touch me but my own hand."

"I'll fix that," Danny promises, tangling one hand into Andrei's hair and pressing the other against the bulge between his legs. "Did you practice like we talked about?"

"I've been opening myself for four days," Andrei says, taking a step backward toward the bed and towing Danny along by the shirt. "Three fingers, pretending they were yours. I can take it, Danny, *please* fuck me." Danny pushes him until he falls on the bed, lowering himself after to catch his mouth in a deep kiss that Andrei returns with vigor.

Andrei hisses as Danny presses into him, fingernails digging into Danny's shoulders, legs cocked wide around his hips. "Oh, it's so much better when it's someone else," he breathes as Danny seats himself fully. "Fuck me, go on, I can take it."

Danny does, starting slow at first but egged on by Andrei's words and hands to a punishing pace. Andrei bites his lip hard against his cries as he comes into his own fist, and the sight of the orgasmic flush on his neck and chest sends Danny tumbling after.

"My coach knows about us," Danny says as he dresses sometime later. Andrei is sprawled across the bed, one fold of the sheet demurely covering his cock. Danny keeps getting distracted from his clothes by the need to touch him.

Andrei hums, considering this. "He's discreet?"

"I trust him," Danny says. "He's known about me for years." He pulls his shirt on and laughs a little. "I think he's worried you'll break my heart."

"Is there a chance of that?" Andrei says sharply. "If there is, we should stop now."

Danny shakes his head. "No offense, you're lovely and all, but no, I'm not in love with you, or in danger of it."

"Good." Danny fishes his sock out from where it had worked itself under the bed. "Fyodor suspects there's someone," Andrei goes on, poking Danny's hip with his toes. "I don't know if he suspects it's you, but if we carry on, he probably will."

"As long as you're not concerned, I'm not concerned," Danny says, tugging his shoes on.

"I'm not concerned," Andrei confirms. "I'm Fyodor's prize student; he's not going to out me."

"Doesn't mean he won't out *me*," Danny points out.

Andrei shrugs. "If he does, I'll just come out anyway. It's the perfect leverage."

"Sweet of you." Danny leans in and kisses him. Andrei turns it a little nasty, licking into his mouth with a proprietary tongue, and Danny is grinning by the time they break apart. "I'm not sure how much time I'll have for the rest of the competition, but I'm glad you came. This was fun."

"If you medal, I'll blow you," Andrei says, smirking. Danny winks and leaves.

He does medal, a nice shiny bronze, and Andrei corners him in the rink bathrooms after the gala with a condom and a grin. "See you in New York," he says, still on his knees in the stall when Danny's catching his breath, lips stretched wide and red. Danny carries the image with him on the long flight back to Bern.

Noemi: https://en.wikipedia.org/wiki/Aromanticism

Noemi: Sorry for the English article

Noemi: But, it's me!

Danny: Oh!

Danny: Thank you for sharing this with me

Noemi: You sound like an after-school special (I love you)

Noemi: Any questions?

Danny: Does it suck having to do the big romantic skates all the time?

Noemi: Sometimes, but mostly no. It's just a performance

Noemi: If people are going to assume things about me, I might as well make them give me medals for it

Danny: Good attitude to have

Danny: Does Noah know?

Noemi: He was the first person I told

Noemi: No offense

Danny: None taken!

Danny: I'm just honored to be on the list at all

Noemi: eyerolling.gif

Noemi: (Seriously. Love you.)

Danny: Love you too, angel

New York is big and bright and loud and Danny *loves* it. Instead of having sex, he drags Andrei out sightseeing their first night there, and comes back loaded down with souvenir tat, as Andrei calls it. "Just because you have no joy in your heart," Danny sniffs. Andrei rolls his eyes but buys a T-shirt from a street vendor.

The competition is stiff at Skate America this year, and Danny knows he'll have a fight to make it to the podium, let alone the Final. His short program goes well enough; he lands all his quads and the judges overscore him a little on the performance components, leaving him in fourth place going into the free.

Andrei, though, delivers a technical masterpiece of a short program, catapulting him into second place behind Sam Kaminsky, the American Dream, and creating a situation in Danny's trousers that he has to cover with his jacket. He sends Andrei a summons by text then and there, and receives a confirmation a few hours later.

When Andrei arrives at Danny's hotel room, Danny is shirtless, and on the bed he's laid out lube, a dental dam, and one of his little black nitrile gloves. He kisses Andrei so hard Andrei melts a little against him, then pulls back and says, "Naked, on your stomach." Andrei raises an eyebrow but obeys.

Danny strips himself down to his briefs and lays himself fully on top of Andrei for a moment, teeth scraping at the back of his neck. When he feels Andrei shudder under him, he starts kissing a path down his spine, hands tights on Andrei's hips until he reaches the swell of his ass, at which point he reaches for the dental dam.

Andrei swears loudly when Danny first licks against him, his shoulders coming up to send his back into a gorgeous arch. "*Fuck*, Danny, do that again," he orders, and Danny obeys, letting his eyes fall shut as he feasts, one of his hands down his briefs to palm and tug at himself.

When Danny has eaten his fill, he puts the dam aside and pulls on the glove, coating his fingers in lube. Andrei takes the first finger easily, with a drawn-out groan that goes straight to Danny's balls. Danny enters him with a second and searches for that spot he'd discovered in Moscow; he knows he's found it when Andrei jolts and curses again.

"Touch yourself," Danny commands. Andrei rocks up onto his knees, one hand disappearing from Danny's view between his legs as Danny fingers him, teeth digging into the meat of Andrei's ass until he comes with a shout, collapsing back down onto the bed.

Andrei knocks the lube aside and rolls over, gasping for breath, a hand pressed to his forehead. Danny stands, pulling his briefs off and climbing onto the bed to straddle Andrei's waist. He sinks down until his ass is against Andrei's spent cock, and Andrei puts his hands on Danny's hips, biting his lip. Danny jerks himself off roughly, grunting and groaning until he spills all over Andrei's chest, come glistening in the valley between his sculpted pecs.

"Well," Andrei says laughingly, running his palm up Danny's chest as he catches his breath. "Out of curiosity, what was it that did it for you?"

"The triple Lutz-loop-triple Sal," Danny admits, trailing his finger through the mess on Andrei's chest.

Andrei smirks. "I'll have to put that combination in more programs, then."

"Only if you want me to die," Danny says. He clambers off Andrei and the man sits up, making for the bathroom to wash himself off.

Danny puts his all into his free skate, and it's enough to scrape him a bronze medal, but not enough to get him to the Final. Andrei pouts at him from his spot on the silver step, and Danny shrugs back, trying not to betray his disappointment. "There's always next year," he says to Nico, trying to convince himself as much as his coach.

Nico pats him on the shoulder. "You'll have plenty of Grand Prix Finals, Danny," he says. "I have faith."

Noemi: Congrats on the bronze!!!

Danny: Thanks!

Danny: And you guys on the gold and silver

Noemi: Thanks babe

Noemi: Shame we won't see you at the Final, though

Noemi: You were robbed in Moscow

Danny: It is what it is

Danny: I'll be watching you guys!

Danny: And we'll have Nationals

Noemi: Yes! Nationals!

Noemi: Another gold for all of us

Danny: Not me

Danny: Valentin's back, like I said he would be

Danny: But I'll happily take a silver

Danny: Dinner beforehand like usual?

Noemi: I can't, I'm being interviewed

Danny: Oho, big shot

Noah: I'll have dinner with you, Danny

Noah: Consolation dinner for those of us not big deals enough to be interviewed

Noemi: If you want to take this piece on women in skating off my hands, be my guest

Danny: Pass

Danny: I don't think they'd appreciate my perspective

Noemi: Haha

Noah: So that's a yes to dinner with me?

Danny: Of course

Noah: Good

Noah: Looking forward to it

Danny: Me too

Chapter 10

THE TRAIN RIDE to Lugano for Nationals is hellishly complex, for all it's only three and a half hours, and Danny is deeply grateful he has no homework to lug through the connections this year. He and his rinkmates arrive at the competition hotel rumpled and irritated, a prickling under Danny's skin that only leaches away under hot water and the notion that he's going to spend the entire evening with Noah.

Back in Bern, he'd packed his best button-down shirt and slacks, all the while telling himself that he wouldn't wear them, that it was just Noah. Giving in to the inevitable in Lugano, he slips into them, fluffing his hair up with the blow-dryer he'd packed in his suitcase, cursing himself for a fool.

Noah meets him in the hotel lobby. Danny notes with no small amount of glee that he isn't the only one who's dressed up tonight; Noah is in a slim black shirt with crisply-pressed trousers, and his hair looks as freshly-washed as Danny's is. He stands when Danny approaches. "Hi," he says, tucking his hands in his back pockets. "What're you hungry for?"

"Well, we're in Ticino," Danny says. "Polenta?"

The polenta is easily found, and they settle into the small restaurant and tuck in. "How have you been?" Danny asks over their food. "I haven't seen much of you this year."

Noah winces. "My fault, I know. I've been busy."

"So have I," Danny says, thinking of Laurin. "It's not all your fault."

Noah smiles at him. "I've been okay," he says. "Working hard with Noemi. I've been trying to figure out if I can manage taking some university classes around skating," he adds, to Danny's surprise.

"What would you go for?" Danny asks. "Biology?"

Noah nods. "I'm not sure I can swing it, but I'd like to try," he says. "Maybe next year." He looks at Danny. "Do you have any interest in university?"

Danny shrugs. "Maybe after I'm retired? It's not a particularly pressing urge. More education would be nice, but it can wait."

"Fair enough."

They wander back to the hotel, pleasantly full, hands in their pockets. Their trek takes them past a liquor store. "Shall we indulge?" Noah asks, slowing down and tilting his head at it.

Well, *this* is new. "Oh, go on, then," Danny says, intrigued. Noah winks. "I'll be right back."

He emerges a few minutes later with a small bottle of red wine. "Acceptable?" he asks, passing it to Danny.

"Perfectly," Danny says, examining the label. "My room?"

Noah agrees and they walk on. Danny calls down for two wine glasses and a bottle opener when they get to his room, and they toast each other. "What's got you in the mood?" Danny asks, settling on the edge of his bed.

Noah drops down next to him. "Not so much in the mood as, why not? Nationals hasn't been much of a challenge for me and Noemi for a couple of years now. Why not take it a little easier?"

"And it's not as though I've got a chance at gold no matter what I do, with Valentin back in the circuit," Danny says, laughing. "Cheers." He taps his glass against Noah's and drinks.

Noah just looks at him, one perfect eyebrow raised. "I think you'd be surprised what you can manage if you set your mind to it, Daniel," he says, an amused tilt to his mouth.

Danny kisses him. The wine and the meal and the closeness of the room and the praise collaborate to drive him a little out of his mind, and he leans forward and kisses Noah, and the important thing, the thing he will cling to in the days to come, is that Noah kisses back. His breath hitches a little bit in surprise, but his lips push back against Danny's, and Danny feels the weight of Noah's hand come to settle on his knee. The kiss ends, and rather than push further, Danny leans back. Noah's eyes are closed, and when he opens them there's that fear again, the one Danny saw in the elevator in January.

"I'm sorry," Danny breathes. "Noah, I'm so sorry—"

"Don't be," Noah says. His hand on Danny's knee gives a little squeeze. Reassurance? "Don't be sorry, Danny." He isn't meeting Danny's eyes.

"Okay," Danny says quietly, and they sit there in silence for a few moments.

"I should go," Noah finally says. He removes his hand from Danny's leg, only to put it briefly on his shoulder. "I have to go. Don't be sorry," he repeats, and then he stands and leaves. Danny hears the door shut behind him and falls back on the bed with a groan, covering his face with his hands and spilling the dregs of his wine on the bedspread. His lips are still tingling where they were pressed against Noah's.

"What's wrong?" Nico asks immediately upon seeing Danny's face the next day for the short program.

"Nothing," Danny says unconvincingly.

"Your head's not in this," Nico says, "I can tell. Tell me what's wrong."

Danny shakes his head. "It's fine, Nico." He can't bring himself to lie to his coach, so he just says again, "It'll be fine. I'm focused, I promise."

"Okay," Nico says doubtfully. His hug before he sends Danny off to center ice is tight, and it does wonders to settle Danny's quivering stomach.

Noemi tracks him down after his performance, dragging him into a quiet corner of the rink. "Something's happened," she says. "Noah was weird all day, and I can tell something's on your mind too. Did anything happen last night?"

Danny bites his lip. It's not outing Noah if he doesn't say

that Noah kissed back, right? "I kissed him," he confesses, driven by the desperate urge to tell *someone*.

Her eyes turn stony. "Is he being an asshole to you about it? I'll kill him, I swear—"

"No," Danny says quickly, putting his hands on her shoulders. "He's not being an asshole about me being gay, I promise. It's not that. It's just...awkward now, you know?"

"No," she says. "I don't."

"Right." Danny winces. "Sorry."

She softens. "It's alright. Awkward is okay, though; awkward is survivable. If he starts being a jerk to you, tell me, and I'll sort him, alright?" He nods and she hugs him. "Get your head in the game," she says, patting him on the cheek. "I want you to give Valentin a run for his money."

"Yes ma'am," he says, and she laughs.

Danny manages to pull himself together enough to clinch silver, a respectable five points behind Valentin. "Good job," the man says to him on the podium as the cameras flash.

"You just had to come back, didn't you?" Danny gripes good-naturedly.

Valentin dimples. "Sorry. Olympics, you know?"

Danny has been trying not to think about the Olympics, but they're close enough now that he can't put it off anymore. He's named to the national team, along with Valentin, obviously, and Mira and Malea for ladies, and Noah and Noemi. Danny gets a little nauseous every time he thinks about it.

Before the Olympics, though, he still has the Euros to get through. Noah is definitely avoiding him this time, and Danny doesn't even try to set something up with him and Noemi like they usually do, instead throwing himself into the public morning practice and thoughts of meeting Andrei late to work out some of his tension.

He's not the only one hard at work during practice; he catches sight of Andrei out of the corner of his eye a handful of times, steadfastly running through his own skates. They're nearing the end of the group ice time when Danny's jolted out of his reverie by the sound of a crash and a familiar voice crying out in pain.

Danny spins toward the sound, as does every skater on the ice, to see Andrei splayed out across it, clutching his leg and biting his lip against the pain. The medics are there in seconds, and all Danny can do is watch as they get him off the ice and out of sight.

Nico meets him with a frown once Danny's done practicing. "Injuries happen," he says. "I know Lebed is a friend, but don't let it rattle you. He's young; he'll bounce back. Keep your head in the game."

"Yes, Nico," Danny says, trying not to think of the unnatural angle of Andrei's foot.

The announcement that Andrei is withdrawing from competition due to injury comes a few hours later, and the competition starts on schedule the next day. Danny still hasn't heard from Andrei, but he forces down his worry and skates his best, coming in third place after the day's events are over. Done with waiting, he pulls his phone out in his room that evening.

Danny: How are you???

Andrei: Broken ankle. I'm out the rest of the season

Andrei: Including the Olympics

Andrei: I could kill myself

Danny: Well, don't do that

Danny: There'll be other Olympics

Danny: What have they said about your recovery?

Andrei: Oh, full recovery, full range of motion back, as long as I stay off it long enough

Andrei: But too damn late to be any good

Andrei: I can't even leave. They want me here for tests for a few days, so we're keeping our original flights out

Danny: Come up to mine

Danny: I'll bet I can distract you

Andrei: I can't move my leg. Don't tempt me

Danny: You don't have to move your leg for me to ride you

Andrei: I'll be there in ten minutes

Andrei is predictably grouchy when he arrives on his little scooter, lower leg encased in a thick cast. Danny lets him in without a word, and Andrei rolls over to the bed. "You'll have to help me get my kit off," he says, hopping off the scooter and sitting on the mattress.

"Fine," Danny says, pulling his shirt off and getting to work on his trouser fly.

Andrei pulls his own shirt off and tosses it aside, eyeing Danny. "I thought I would be the one in the worse mood here," he says, "but you look more pissed off than me, and I didn't think that was possible. It's a little refreshing, to be honest."

Danny sighs, kicking his briefs away and sitting carefully next to him so as not to jostle his leg. "At myself," he says. "I didn't offer just for your sake." He smiles ruefully at Andrei.

"Good," Andrei says. "I don't want your pity sex. What'd you do?"

"Kissed someone I shouldn't've," Danny says. "Ruined a good friendship."

Andrei frowns at him, then reaches out and pushes a hand into Danny's hair. "Take it out on me, then," he says, a hint of a challenge in his voice. Danny kisses him, the tension leaving his body in a rush as Andrei licks into his mouth and tugs at his hair.

Together they get Andrei out of his trousers and underwear and on his back on the bed. Danny opens himself a little more roughly than he usually does; he's in a hurry, and the burn scratches the itch under his skin. Andrei strokes himself while Danny works, rolling a condom on when Danny passes it to him. Once he's stretched enough, Danny straddles Andrei's hips, takes hold of his cock, and sinks down onto it.

"Oh, Christ, I needed this," he says in a relieved rush, bottoming out. "It's been a hellish month and a half."

"Happy to—*fuck*—happy to oblige," Andrei bites out as Danny starts to rock on top of him. "Couldn't find somebody else in the meantime? That's surprising."

"No time," Danny says. "Nico's been cracking the whip about the Olympics."

"Don't fucking remind me," Andrei grinds out, and Danny laughs.

"Sorry," he says, leaning down to put his back into the way he's fucking himself on Andrei's cock. "Don't *thrust*," he says a minute later, putting his hand on Andrei's hip to hold him down. "You're not meant to be moving your leg."

"Nag nag nag," Andrei gripes, but he stills. "Can I at least touch you?"

"Yeah," Danny says, leaning up. "Yeah, Andrei, touch me."

With Andrei's hand tugging at his cock, it's not long at all before Danny is able to eke out an orgasm, shuddering and spilling over Andrei's chest. He slips Andrei out of him and settles beside him, jerking him off through the condom while Andrei sucks on his tongue. Andrei bites him when he comes. "Sorry," he hisses, panting.

"It's okay," Danny says, licking at the painful spot. He drops down onto his back next to Andrei, listening to him catch his breath.

"For the record," Andrei says after a while, flipping his hand up to land on Danny's chest. "That person you kissed is an idiot. It's hard to imagine the sort of person who wouldn't love you."

"You don't love me," Danny points out mildly.

Andrei smirks at him. "I'm hard to imagine," he murmurs, and Danny laughs.

Eventually they get up and wrangle Andrei back into his clothes. Andrei puts his hands on Danny's shoulders as Danny is tugging his sock onto his good foot. "This thing about me not loving you," he says haltingly. "It's not…It's not *you*; you know that, right?" He bites his lip. "I don't think…I don't think I'm capable of loving. Not like that."

"I know," Danny assures him. "And there's a word for that." Andrei lifts an eyebrow. "Aromanticism," Danny says, switching to English for the one word. "Means people who don't love others romantically."

"Huh," Andrei says, eyes going distant for a moment. "How about that."

"I'll send you some links," Danny says, tying off Andrei's shoelace. "There. All set."

"Thanks." Danny helps Andrei onto his little scooter and Andrei kisses him. "Good luck with your friend," he says.

"Good luck with your ankle," Danny tells him. "I'll get the door." He swats Andrei on the ass as he leaves, making the other skater snort, and shuts the door feeling much better than he had an hour ago.

Chapter 11

"I'M GONNA HAVE to spend this whole thing drunk, aren't I?" Danny murmurs to Noemi on the plane to British Columbia, desperately not looking back at where Noah has traded seats with a luger, presumably to get away from Danny.

"Not if you'd let me murder him with one of my skates," Noemi murmurs back pleasantly, sipping the first class complimentary champagne. "He's being such an asshole."

"Then you'd be out a partner, and I'd never see you at a competition again," Danny points out. "No, best to drink."

She pats his hand. "You just need to find yourself a Village boyfriend," she says. "Someone to take your mind off things."

"Mmm, say more," Danny purrs. He can't say that he would have had one lined up, save for a broken ankle. *Poor Andrei*, he thinks, and makes a resolution to text the other skater everything he misses.

"I'm serious," Noemi insists. "Some big jock with biceps the size of your head."

"This is the Winter Olympics, darling," he points out. "More likely to be his leg muscles that are huge."

"I don't think you're taking this seriously," she sniffs. He laughs.

Danny gives her words a little more weight when they actually make it to the Village and he gets a good look at some of the bodies on display there. There's one man in particular, broad-shouldered and well-built, with messy black hair and piercing dark eyes, who gives Danny the once-over in return when they go for a drink. Bold and unashamed; just Danny's type. Danny tips him a wink and turns back to what Noemi's been saying.

He sees the man again in the crush after the opening ceremonies, and Danny is aware enough through the haze of excitement to take note of which delegation he's with. Armenia; Danny will have to remember that.

There's a huge party in the Village after the openers, and Danny is only a little bit surprised when the body that appears at his side through the crowd at the bar belongs to the mystery Armenian. "Let me get you a drink," the man yells in English in Danny's ear over the noise.

"Just a soda," Danny calls back. "Trying to keep a clear head tonight." The man nods, a gleam in his eye, and flags one of the bartenders over.

Danny catches Noemi's eye and points at the man; she toasts him, a clear approval, and he and the Armenian fight their way to a quiet corner. "What's your name?" Danny asks once they're settled in chairs by a fake fire pit.

"Vardan," the man says. "I'm a snowboarder," which was going to be Danny's next question.

"I'm Danny," Danny says, but before he can go on, Vardan holds up a hand.

"Let me guess," he says. "Figure skater?"

"What gave me away?" Danny asks, laughing.

Vardan grins. "Powerful thighs, not enough bulk for ice hockey, plus you move like a dancer."

Danny crosses one leg over the other, flexing. "I'm glad my thighs pass muster." Vardan laughs. He has a good laugh, loud and resonant and unashamed, like his flirting.

They talk for another hour, bantering and joking, long past the point when their glasses are empty, and then Vardan leans close and says, "Forgive me for shooting my shot, but do you want to get out of here?"

"Shot landed," Danny says. "Let's go."

Vahe's lodgings aren't far away from where the party is, and they race there through the biting Canadian air. There's a bowl of Olympics-branded condoms in the lobby of his building.

Danny raises an eyebrow at Vardan and, at his nod, loads his pockets up.

"Can I kiss you?" Vardan asks as soon as the door is shut behind them. "I've been dying to ever since I saw you the other day." Danny nods, eager as a boy, and Vahe gets his big hands on Danny's face and pulls him in.

He's a good kisser, quite possibly the best Danny has ever kissed. He's bold but not pushy, leaving Danny enough room to give as good as he gets, and his arms wrap Danny up tight and warm, their bodies pressing together in a way that makes Danny gasp into his mouth. He's also taller than Danny is, by quite a bit, and Danny lets his head tip back in delight as they kiss.

Vardan asks for permission before every article of clothing he takes off Danny's body, until Danny is moaning his assent every time he opens his mouth. Danny gets Vardan down to his boxers in turn, and when he gets consent and works them over Vardan's hips, he looks down and his jaw drops open.

Vardan laughs, almost a giggle. "Your eyes just dilated like a cat's."

"Holy *shit*," Danny breathes, looking back up at his face. "Are you serious?"

"I get that a lot," Vardan says. "I understand if you don't want to, er, *receive*. Most people don't."

"Oh no," Danny says immediately, shaking his head. "That is going inside me. We may have to work up to it, but I am sitting on that."

Vardan kisses him, sharp and sweet. "Call me an optimist, but I came prepared."

"Prepared?" Danny asks, a little breathless from the kiss. "What does that mean?"

Apologetically, Vardan steps back from Danny, walking over to his suitcase. He pulls a small case from inside and unzips it, showing its contents to Danny: three dildos, increasing in size and girth, the biggest just barely thinner than what Vardan has between his legs.

Danny blinks. "Remind me where you're from again?"

"Armenia," Vardan says, lips twitching.

"Heaven?" Danny asks. Vardan laughs one of his good laughs again. "Get over here," Danny says, pointing to the bed. "We have work to do."

Danny: [img]

Danny: Wish you were here

Andrei: Absolutely shut up

Andrei: That's a prosthetic

Danny: Nope

Danny: As I have spent the last four days discovering, thrillingly real

Andrei: UGH

Andrei: I'm furious with you

Andrei: Never speak to me again

Danny: The Olympics is great so far

Danny: Having a fine time

Andrei: How dare you

Danny: Gotta go

Danny: I promised to suck it in exchange for the picture

Andrei: I hope you choke on it

Danny: :-*

Danny introduces Vardan to Noemi; they get on like a house on fire. He drags her to all the snowboarding events they can fit around their practice schedules, and he's there when Vardan wins the gold. When Danny asks him what he wants as a prize, he very politely asks if Danny wouldn't mind sitting on his face. Danny most certainly does *not* mind.

He can't help but see Noah during practice and publicity events, but for the most part they don't interact. Noah does catch his eye once and give him an awkward but seemingly heartfelt smile; Danny returns it, a little hopeful for the first time that maybe their friendship can survive one kiss, once Noah's over his gay panic.

Danny takes Vardan's cock on the seventh day after the opening ceremonies, when he has minimal skate time the next day and they've had the chance to put all three of Vardan's dildos to good use. "Ohhhhh," he breathes into Vardan's forehead, clutching at his shoulders like he's dying. "Oh, Vardan, you'll ruin me for all other cocks."

Vardan kisses his chest and holds still, like a good horse-hung man, as Danny starts to work himself back and forth. "*Fuck*," Danny bites out. To distract himself, he asks, "How long has it been since you've topped?"

"About two years," Vardan says, leaning forward to press his lips to Danny's neck and suck lightly. "I had a good feeling about this Olympics, though."

"Lucky me," Danny pants wickedly.

He prides himself on the fact that he gets Vardan to come inside him before letting himself give in. It's by far the most mind-bending orgasm he's ever had with a partner, the thickness of Vardan's cock inside him as he clenches around it so solid and *big* that Danny almost passes out. He comes to cradled in Vardan's arms, tucked against his chest, and sighs happily.

Andrei texts him the night before the short program, a simple *Stay focused* that settles Danny more than Nico's pep talk. Vardan kisses him firmly in a dark corner, promising to be in the stands for both programs; they've agreed to no sex between the short and free, to keep Danny sharp.

"Are you ready?" Nico asks him, rinkside. Danny nods. "Then there's nothing more to say." Nico pulls him into a hug. "Go on."

Danny goes, and he does really, shockingly well. He's in fifth place after the short, *somehow*, and Noemi jumps on him as soon as he's out of the kiss-and-cry. "You're amazing!" she shouts in his ear, and he grins and squeezes her tight.

She and Noah are in third place after their compulsory and short dances. Between time with her and time with Vardan and practice, Danny barely has a moment to think before the day of the free skate dawns.

To his surprise, Valentin Wolf finds him in the warm-up area as he's stretching. "I just wanted to say good luck," he says, holding out his hand. Danny shakes it, taken aback. "This is my last Olympics," the man goes on, "but I'm glad I'll be leaving Switzerland in such capable hands."

"Thank you," Danny says, stunned. "I don't know what to say." Valentin claps him on the shoulder, smiles, and returns to his own warm-ups.

He pulls out a fifth-place finish, pushing himself on the ice until he has to fall to his knees and gasp with exertion once he drops his final pose. It's not a medal, but it's enough to satisfy him. Nico beams when his scores are announced, thumping him on the back, and Danny grins, exhausted but pleased.

Andrei texts him that night.

Andrei: Congratulations!

Danny: Thanks!

Danny: Not a medal but I'll take it, haha

Andrei: Next Olympics is going to be a completely different animal

Andrei: You'll medal for sure

Danny: Don't jinx me

Andrei: I'm serious

Andrei: Kaminsky, Tsvetkov, Wolf…They'll all be gone

Andrei: Retired

Andrei: It'll just be us, at the top of the sport, better than they ever were

Danny: You make it sound so certain

Andrei: I am certain

Andrei: I'm coming back stronger next season

Andrei: I already have plans

Danny: Of course you do

Danny: Don't push yourself too hard too soon, Andrei

Andrei: I know my limits, Danny

Andrei: You don't have to worry about me

Andrei: I'll be there next season

Danny: I wasn't worried

Andrei: Good

Their events done, Danny, Vardan, and Noemi catch as many of the other sports as they can fit into their schedules. "I'm in the wrong game," Danny says, breathless after a neck-and-neck speed skating race that ends in an Olympic record. "Tell Nico I'm switching to speed skating."

"Don't you dare," Noemi says, laughing. Danny kisses her on the temple and resumes cheering loudly for the medalists.

Danny abandons his lodgings and spends all his nights with Vardan. They don't fuck every night, but it's unspeakably nice to fall asleep wrapped in his arms, his breath on Danny's forehead or the back of his neck. Nico lets him be, busy wining and dining sponsors on his behalf in the wake of his fifth-place finish.

"I'll miss you," Danny says on the last night, straddling Vardan in their bed. "You've made this Olympics an amazing time."

"I'll miss you too, my dear," Vardan says, running his hands up and down Danny's thighs. "But we'll keep in touch. I don't intend to lose you as a friend just because we can't be lovers anymore."

Danny leans down to kiss him and lets Vardan roll him

over, and they make love one last time, Danny shuddering his orgasm into Vardan's hand before taking him into his mouth. He sleeps on his side, Vardan's arm thrown over his waist, and when Danny leaves to meet Nico and the rest of Team Switzerland for their flight, it's with the taste of Vardan's lips still on his tongue.

"Well?" Nico asks in the airport as they wait for boarding. "How was your first Olympics?"

"Incredible," Danny says. "I want to do it again."

"You will," Nico tells him, patting him on the shoulder. "Four years and you'll be back. We'll make sure you medal next time, too."

"I can't wait."

Chapter 12

DANNY GETS HOME from the Olympics only to dive headlong into training for Worlds. "You can't let up just because the Olympics are over," Nico tells him countless times. "End the season on that same high."

"Yes, Nico," Danny replies every time, his legs and lungs aching from Lutz after loop after Salchow.

Worlds is in Italy this year, and Noemi sends him no less than seven swimsuits for his approval before she finally settles on one. He doubts he'll have time for swimming between ice time, but maybe the hotel has a pool. He winds up with two new pairs himself.

Turin is close enough to Bern that they take the train rather than fly. "Feels like we're going to Nationals," he murmurs to Nico beside him.

"Watch that mindset," his coach says mildly. "This is a much harder competition than Nationals." Danny sighs and balls up his jacket to try and catch some sleep.

Andrei texts him incessantly throughout the day of the short programs, even more once the skating is done and Danny is in a comfortable fourth. Danny answers when he can, but there's only so many formulations of *Yes, I am focused* that he can come up with. And besides that, Noemi is at his side constantly when neither of them are on the ice.

"Rumor has it they're axing the compulsory *and* the original for next season," she says to him over dinner the night after the men's short. Noah is, of course, nowhere to be seen, but in fairness, Danny isn't sure Noemi invited him in the first place. She's almost as hacked off at him as Danny is. "What they're going to replace it with I have no idea, of course, because why should we be given enough time to prepare?"

Danny makes soothing noises and redirects conversation to Nadja's heroes, the Canadian ice dancing pair that's slated to take the gold for about the dozenth time. "The rumors *I* hear are that they're trying for a world record tomorrow," he says, and she's off again, this time with a glint in her eyes.

He really should be training during the original dance, since it's only a few hours before his own free skate, but he manages to slip away from Nico to watch the group that has both his friends and the Canadians. The latter do set a world record, pure artistry in motion, but Noah and Noemi pull out a clean second-place finish, settling them nicely going into their next event. Danny stays long enough to hug Noemi and wave awkwardly at Noah, who lights up when he sees him, before he has to go back or be murdered by Nico.

"You have to stop doing that," Nico tells him crossly when he finds him again. "Your performance comes first."

"I wasn't going to miss a chance to watch a world record being set," Danny says. "It inspires me." Nico rolls his eyes but holds his tongue, and Danny sets himself to running through his footwork in the hallway.

To his surprise, he sees Noah and Noemi in the stands when he takes the ice, waving Swiss flags at him. He laughs, hugs Nico, and goes and nets himself a small silver and his first Worlds medal, a nice shiny bronze.

"Proud of you," Nico says, thumping him on the back in the kiss-and-cry. "Next time, higher on the podium."

"Yes, Coach," Danny says, just to be contrary, and Nico laughs.

There are rounds and rounds of interviews after the medals ceremony, soundbite after soundbite for various sports media outlets. He's taking a moment to himself in the rink bathroom afterward, washing his face and enjoying the silence, when he hears the door open and then the lock click shut.

Noah is standing there when he turns around. "There you

are," he says, smiling when Danny meets his gaze. "I've been looking everywhere for you." He takes a step closer. "I wasn't sure Noemi was going to let me near you," he goes on. His eyes are flickering all over Danny's face like he can't decide where to look. "She's very protective of me," Danny says. "And you've been kind of an asshole lately."

Noah winces. "I know. And I'm sorry, really I am. You deserved better than how I treated you." He takes another step closer. "I wanted to say congratulations on your medal."

"And to you for yours," Danny says, just to be polite, but congratulating him doesn't require locking the door and he knows it, and Noah knows he knows it, and he takes another step closer.

"I also wanted to do this," Noah says, and he raises one hand and cups it around Danny's jaw. He leans in, hovering a heartbeat away for permission, and when Danny lets his eyes fall shut Noah closes the gap and kisses him.

It's a soft kiss, gentle to start, but when Danny inhales a sharp breath Noah kisses him again, deeper, his other hand settling on Danny's hip. Danny balls his fists into Noah's shirt and chases after him, his knees going a little weak. Noah grins against his lips and gets both their mouths open, making a little sound of pleasure at the first touch of Danny's tongue that goes straight to Danny's heart.

They make out for some length of time that Danny can't *possibly* be expected to keep track of, and Noah's lips are red and bitten when they finally pull apart. "I'm not in a position to offer you anything serious," he says quietly, brushing Danny's cheek with his thumb. "For a long time I thought that meant I couldn't offer you anything at all. But I figured out eventually that it should probably be your decision. I like you a lot, and from the way you were kissing me just now you like me too, and it seems a shame to waste that, if you're willing."

Danny bites his lip, considering it for a long moment. It's not what he wants—or rather, it's not *all* of what he wants. But it's Noah's hands on his face and his waist, Noah's mouth on his, Noah's time spent with him again. And it's probably a good idea not to get too serious too soon while they're both still closeted. So after a minute of thought, he says, "Alright. Let's try casual, then. We'll see how it goes."

"You're comfortable with that?" Noah asks, his eyes searching.

Danny nods. "Exclusive or non-exclusive?"

A flicker of a frown crosses Noah's face. "Non, I would say."

"And *you're* comfortable with that?" Danny probes.

"I am," Noah says. "Exclusivity implies a lot of things. Like you said, we're trying this casually."

"Alright," Danny says. He's smiling, a little giddy, and Noah's dark eyes are molten. He tips his forehead against Noah's, and Noah pulls his chin up to kiss him again.

"We should probably leave separately," Noah says after a few more breathless minutes.

"I know the drill," Danny says with a smile. "You go. I'll take five minutes to make myself look less kissed and then I'll be out. And I'll tell Noemi we've made up so she gets off your back. I take it you're not out to her?" he adds.

Noah shakes his head. "I know it's not fair to ask you to keep secrets from her," he starts, but Danny holds up a hand.

"First rule is, I don't out people. We'll keep it between us."

"Alright," Noah says. "Thank you." Another kiss, a lingering touch at Danny's waist, and he's gone, leaving Danny to splash cold water on his face and try to stop grinning.

Winter slips into spring, and Danny slips into his off-season training program, more familiar than some of his clothes at this point. As always, Nico keeps him busy, between conditioning, jump drills, and runs, but he and Noah make time to see each other every other week or so. Between their dates and his friend-dates with Noemi, some of which now include Noah again, Danny's personal time is just as busy as his training schedule.

Most of the time, his dates with Noah are just long enough for a quick meal together, or a hurried makeout, but one day in June both their calendars are wide open from dawn until noon the next day. Danny packs a bag and heads to Noah's just after breakfast, where he's greeted with a deep kiss and a promising hand on his ass.

The kissing progresses to the couch, Danny stretched out under Noah where he can hook a leg around his hip and draw him closer. When Noah goes to take Danny's shirt off, Danny notices that his hands are shaking.

He catches one and brings it to his mouth for a kiss, then puts his other hand on Noah's cheek. "Hey," he says, and Noah looks at him, nerves clearly written across his face. "Is this your first time?" Danny asks quietly. "I should have asked first."

Noah shakes his head. "I did some experimenting, to confirm things. I know what I'm doing."

"Then what is it?"

Noah sighs, his expression changing to a rueful smile. "It's stupid." Danny waits, and Noah butts his forehead up against his and says, "It's just, it's *you*, you know?"

Danny has to kiss him for that. "Exactly," he murmurs. "It's just me."

"Right," Noah says, exhaling a shaky breath. "It's just you and me." When he goes back to the hem of Danny's shirt, his hands are steadier.

Noah buries his face in Danny's neck when he comes, more often than not, and he touches Danny like he's made of gold, respectfully and gently—a little *too* gently; Danny has to carefully coax him into being a little rougher sometimes. The first time he yanks on Danny's hair and calls him *Daniel* in a sharp tone, Danny comes on the spot. Once they're done laughing, Noah says he gets the picture, and from then on, his hands are never far from Danny's hair during sex, pulling or twisting or just carding through the strands.

Andrei gets the go-ahead to go back on the ice in late June, much to his relief. He calls Danny after his first week back in full-time training, voice flushed with victory. "I have big plans this season," he says again. "Promise you'll watch me if we're not at the same Grand Prix events."

"Of course I'll watch you," Danny says. "I watch everyone."

"No," Andrei says, "promise you'll watch *me*. It would be better if you were there in person, but I can't guarantee that, so you have to promise to watch."

"I promise," Danny says. "No chance you'll tell me what you're planning?"

"It's a surprise," Andrei tells him, and that's all he'll say, no matter how Danny pushes.

Nico asks for his input on choreography in mid-July, and all Danny wants to do is push for more sensuality, more sex. Nico, to his surprise, goes for it, and they put together a short program that Danny knows he'll have to tell his parents not to watch, or at least not to discuss with him. "It fits your mood this summer," Noemi says drily when he tells her about it, which is how Danny discovers Noah accidentally left a mark high enough on his neck to be seen. She doesn't ask who it's from, though, just pats him on the shoulder and congratulates him on the sex.

Andrei must have multiple surprises planned, because the first one comes in early August, via text.

Andrei: [img]

Danny: Oh my God!

Danny: RED

Danny: I love it!!!

Andrei: Do you?

Andrei: You don't think it's too much?

Danny: It's perfect

Danny: Seriously, it looks so good

Danny: The color suits you

Danny: The Red Swan of Russia

Andrei: I want to redo my whole image with this comeback

Andrei: An entirely different skater

Danny: I can't wait

Danny: Are your programs done?

Andrei: Still working out specifics for my free

Andrei: I want to push as far as possible

Danny: Leave some for the rest of us

Andrei posts a picture of his new red hair a few days later, styled a little differently, and the skating blogs go *wild*. Danny compiles every thirsty comment and sends them to Andrei in a daily digest; Andrei thanks him after a week by talking him through a toe-curling orgasm as he details every suggestion from the comments he wants to do to Danny when they're together again.

Lying in bed with Noah on his twentieth birthday in mid-August, sweat cooling off their skin and hands tangled together, Danny murmurs, "I don't think I've ever been happier."

Noah kisses his hair and tightens his arm around Danny's shoulders. "Me either," he murmurs back. Danny props his chin on Noah's chest and looks up at him; he's smiling, gorgeous in the post-orgasm flush Danny has come to relish so much.

"We're gonna be great this season," Danny says. "You and me and Noemi, we'll be amazing. I can feel it."

Noah taps him lightly on the nose. "You're always amazing." Danny rolls his eyes, fighting a blush, and Noah grins and says, "But you're right. This is going to be a very good season. I can't wait to see what we come up with."

His hand runs softly through Danny's hair, the other stroking lightly over the skin of his upper back. Danny is hardening again at the touches, a birthday miracle, and from the look in Noah's eye, he can tell. Danny presses a kiss to his side, and then to his nipple, and then to his collarbone, and then Noah is pulling him into his lap to kiss his mouth as Danny straddles his waist. "A very good season indeed," Danny pauses to murmur, and then dives back in.

Chapter 13

ANDREI'S TEXT COMES in just before Group Two of Skate Canada takes the ice for the short program.

Andrei: Are you watching?

Danny: I promised

Danny: This better be impressive

Andrei: It will be

Andrei's skating fifth in Group Two. He looks *good* as he takes the ice, Danny notes, with his new hair color and cut and a costume designed to make him look like a comet. Just as ravishing as he had been blond, but more fiery, more alive.

The music starts, and at first Danny can't tell what Andrei's big surprise is going to be. It's Andrei, so it's a stunning program, technically perfect, but that's hardly surprising at this point—and then Andrei goes into a jump entry that Danny can't quite understand until Andrei's flying through the air, and then he's landed and Danny's hands are over his mouth.

A quad Lutz.

A quad Lutz. It's never been done before. No one's even *tried* it before, and here Andrei Lebed's done it as easy as breathing.

Danny is on the phone to Nico as soon as Andrei's off the ice, even before his scores are read out. "I need it, Nico," he says as soon as his coach pics up.

"You can't," Nico says baldly. "You need to focus on your programs as they exist currently, especially if you want a hope of beating that boy now he has it. You need perfection, Danny;

we don't have time to train you on something new and still experimental."

"I can't beat him without it," Danny counters. His fingers are knotted anxiously into his shirt and he's pacing his apartment, quick fevered steps over the hardwood.

He hears Nico start to say something, then stop and sigh. "Danny," he says, his voice suddenly very serious. "I need you to be honest with me. If I say no, are you going to do it behind my back?"

"Probably," Danny admits without a shred of shame.

"Then fine. Bring me solid video footage of the jump, and we'll dedicate the last half an hour of your practice times to trying it. But *no more*. I need you focused on your programs as is. Deal?"

"Deal," Danny says. "Thank you." His phone is buzzing with another call. "I have to go, I have to take this. *Thank you*, Nico."

"Thank me by not breaking your leg," Nico grumbles, but fondly. Danny hangs up on him and accepts the other call.

"Did you see?" Andrei's voice is triumphant. "I did it."

"I saw," Danny says, grinning. "How are you on the phone right now? You should be in a million interviews at once."

"I wanted to talk to you first." Danny can hear his grin. "*I did it*, Danny."

"You did."

"You have to be at the Final," Andrei says. "Promise me."

"I'll do my best."

"Fuck your best. *Promise me*."

"Alright, alright," Danny says, laughing. "I promise. I'm proud of you."

"Fyodor's proud of me too," Andrei says. "He's frowning a lot, but I can tell."

"He should be," Danny tells him. "Now get off the phone and do your interviews, history maker."

"Yes, sir," Andrei drawls, in a tone of voice that makes it *very* clear what Danny has waiting for him at the Final.

He earns his place there by late November, a silver in China and a surprising gold in Russia clinching his spot. Noah and

Noemi are going too, two golds under their belts; the mood in their get-together just after the Bompard is so triumphant that Danny winds up buying three rounds of shots and blowing Noah's back out in bed that night, both of them drunkenly giggling with glee and victory into their kisses as they catch their breath afterward.

By the time they land in Beijing for the Final, Danny is landing the quad Lutz about forty percent of the time, and is waging a quiet but persistent war with Nico to let him put it in his free skate. "We'll see how things stand after the short," Nico finally concedes the day before. Danny quietly fist-pumps to himself and Nico rolls his eyes.

Danny's nerves are uncharacteristically short during his warm-up the next day, making him twitchy and snappish, even with Nico. His coach puts him in a quiet corner, away from all the other skaters, and directs him through stretch after stretch until he can open his water bottle without wanting to throw it against the wall.

"You have a solid short program," Nico says when they're finally rinkside. "Do it perfectly and you'll be in fine shape for the free."

"Oh, that's all?" Danny says sarcastically before he can stop himself.

"You've done it perfectly countless times before," Nico tells him, putting a hand on the back of his neck. "Just do it one more time." He gives him a little shake and then pushes him out onto the ice proper.

Danny, somehow, does it perfectly. The nervous, wired feeling running through his blood is *perfect* for the sex appeal of his short program, it turns out, and although his quad Salchow is a little wobbly, it's a clean landing, fully scored. At the end of the day, he's in second place. Ahead of him is only Andrei, another clean quad Lutz in his short that had the crowd cheering.

Over dinner, Danny stares wide-eyed at Nico, unblinking, until Nico finally snaps, "Alright. Land it twice cleanly in practice the day of, and I'll let you put it in. *Cleanly*, mind you."

"I love you, Nico," Danny says. "I can win this.'

"I know you can."

The short dance had been before the men's free, and after dinner he spends hours in Noah's room with him and Noemi, dissecting all their competition. Danny's friends are in a precarious first, less than a point away from the team from France that had finished with the small silver. Their free is after his the next day. "I'll be there, no matter what," he promises.

"With a gold medal on," Noemi says. Danny drops her a wink over the churning of his stomach.

He runs through his free skate once during morning practice before turning his attention to the real task. Without thinking about it too much, moving almost casually, he builds up speed, turns into his entrance, and pushes himself off the ice, spinning and landing without a wobble.

He turns to look at Nico, who nods approvingly and holds up one finger.

Andrei is looking at him as he starts building up speed again; out of the corner of his eye, Danny sees him skate to a halt to watch. *How's this, Andrei?* Danny thinks to himself, and jumps it again.

"A deal's a deal," Nico says after practice is done. "Put it in."

"I won't let you down," Danny promises, standing and stretching.

"You're not capable of letting me down," Nico says. Danny looks at him, startled. "I won't be disappointed in you, whatever happens," Nico tells him. "Don't do it for me. Do it for you. Do it to prove to yourself you can."

Danny nods solemnly. He can do that.

Being in second place, he's skating second-to-last, and that leaves him a nice long time to warm up and try to drown out the sounds of the crowd cheering for the other four skaters. Andrei is once again in his periphery, jogging up and down the corridors with an intense look in his eye. Danny blocks him out and keeps stretching his hamstrings.

The replacement jump composition he and Nico have worked out changes his quad Salchow just before the halfway mark into a Lutz. His first jump, his trademark triple flip, goes smoothly, and he goes into the quad Lutz with confidence, plenty of speed, and a perfect entrance.

It isn't enough. He wipes out, landing on his side and rolling. Practice gets him back on his feet in moments, and he goes on autopilot into his contingency, adding a combination onto his triple loop in the second half. It's not bad. His scores, when he gets them, are good. If it were anyone other than Andrei waiting for their music to start, he might have won.

But it is Andrei, and Andrei has come back from injury as a powerhouse, the likes of which Danny has honestly never seen. His free skate is sheer perfection, the quad Lutz somehow still flawless as the first jump in his program.

Nico is looking at him worriedly when Danny comes back to himself, and he musters up a reassuring smile for his coach. "It's alright," he says. "He earned it."

Nico visibly relaxes. "That he did, lad. Hell of a skater." He claps for Andrei's scores, and Danny does the same.

"Hell of a skater," Danny echoes.

The silver around his neck really does feel quite good, he decides on the podium. He can be happy with it, for now. And what feels better is Andrei's hand around his forearm as they climb down after the photo op, and the way he leans forward to murmur, "We both have to skate tomorrow, but after?"

"After the gala," Danny confirms. "I have a few hours before we fly out." He drops Andrei a wink. "Champion's choice." Andrei's eyes gleam.

Danny's exhibition skate this year is more of the same as his short program, lust and sauciness, a thin white button-down open halfway down his chest. It does plenty to put him in the mood, and Andrei's exhibition does the rest, his gleaming red hair flying about his head, exposing the long line of his neck as he spins.

Andrei plasters himself to Danny's back as Danny fumbles his hotel room door open, and they're on each other before it closes, tearing at each other's clothes and kissing hungrily. "Have you decided what you wanted?" Danny asks, laughing as Andrei almost pops a button loose in his haste to get his shirt off. "I want to ride you," Andrei says, voice low and raspy. "Can I?"

"Absolutely," Danny says, working his trousers and briefs down over his hips.

Andrei stretches himself, kneeling over Danny while Danny tends to his own erection. "I did a little bit before the gala," he says, face screwed up in concentration. "Just need to, *ah*, refresh things." Once the condom is on, Danny wraps his hand around Andrei's cock, not stroking, just holding it loosely. "Fuck," Andrei says eloquently. "I'm ready."

Andrei tosses his head back as he sinks down on Danny's cock, his thighs flexing and his head falling back. "You're fucking stunning," Danny bites out, just in case Andrei doesn't know. Andrei looks down at him, laughing, only to cry out as Danny snaps his hips up, pushing the rest of the way inside him.

True to his word, Danny lets Andrei set the pace, and soon they're both grunting and groaning as their bodies slap together, Danny's hands digging bruises into Andrei's hips. "Fuck, your cock feels so good," Andrei breathes. "Pull my hair?" Danny gets his fingers into the red strands and tugs, and Andrei gasps, one hand moving to strip over his own cock.

"Fuck, Danny, harder, make me come," Andrei demands. Danny hauls himself forward to sink his teeth into Andrei's shoulder, hips pistoning even harder into him, and when that doesn't do it he reaches one hand around to where his cock is splitting Andrei open, pressing the pads of two of his fingers against Andrei's stretched rim.

Andrei comes with a shocked cry, jerking and splashing onto Danny's chest. A few more thrusts and Danny is gone too, falling back against the pillows with a breathless sigh. "Fuck, that was good," he manages after a few seconds, rubbing both hands across his face.

Andrei leans down and kisses him. "It's always good with you," he says, shockingly sweet, before lifting himself off Danny's cock and groaning. "Thank you. I needed this."

"Anytime," Danny says, and rolls himself to his feet to make for the bathroom.

Chapter 14

NATIONALS IS ALMOST an anticlimax after the emotional roller coaster that was the Grand Prix Final. But Danny texts with Noah and Noemi the whole ride up, and he's able to muster up some excitement by the time they get to Zug. "Can I do the quad Lutz?" he asks Nico as they wait for a cab.

"You don't need it," Nico says. "I don't want you risking injury for points you don't need when your technical base score is ten points higher than anyone else's."

"It'll be good practice for the Euros," Danny counters. "And if I fall, my advantage is high enough that I'll probably still medal."

"You could fall twice and still win," Nico says. "That doesn't mean risking your neck makes sense."

"Any time I jump, I risk my neck," Danny points out. "I don't want to slow my momentum down for Nationals only to have to pick it back up in January."

They argue the whole way to the hotel, and to Danny's surprise, he wins. "If you really think you can do it, then I suppose I won't stand in your way," Nico relents, patting Danny on the shoulder in the hotel elevator. "Just promise me you'll use some sense."

"I promise," Danny says, too surprised and relieved to try and argue that he's always sensible.

He hasn't had any real time with Noah since before the Final, and as they laugh and chatter with Noemi in her room, it's a real fight to keep himself from jumping the man. Noah feels similarly, to judge from the way his eyes keep flickering to Danny and the way his hand keeps finding its way to Danny's knee.

They don't get any time alone that night, but Danny drags Noah into a supply closet at the rink for a hurried makeout between their events. "God, I've missed you," Noah hisses, kissing Danny as fiercely as he can without leaving any visible sign.

"Tomorrow," Danny whispers, tipping his head back for Noah to trail his lips up his neck. "I'll come to your room tomorrow, after everything's done."

"I want to be inside you," Noah breathes, and every nerve in Danny's body lights up in excitement. They haven't done that yet; Noah expressed some hesitation about topping when the idea was first broached over the summer, and Danny hasn't wanted to push. "Please, Danny, can I fuck you tomorrow night?" Noah goes on, one hand on Danny's lower back and the other cupping his ass.

"Fuck, Noah," Danny says reverently, catching his mouth to bite gently at his lower lip. "Of course you can. If you're sure."

"I'm sure," Noah says. He kisses Danny again, all lips and tongue, and then presses their foreheads together. "God, you're going to be the death of me," he murmurs, his mouth curved up in a sweet little smile that makes Danny's heart beat even faster.

"Only the little death," Danny says, and Noah laughs, too loud for their rendezvous.

They take that as their cue to stop, sneaking out of the closet and back to their respective coaches. Danny somehow lands a quad Lutz in his short with the remnants of that erection, and he makes a mental note to himself to kiss Noah senseless before every performance. It seems to be good luck.

He lands it the next day too, and wins the gold by an impressive margin. "Well done," Nico tells him after the medal ceremony, and that feels almost as good as the weight of the ribbon around his neck. "I want to stay and watch Noah and Noemi," he says, rubbing at the metal circle absentmindedly.

Nico goes back to the hotel, so he isn't there when Noah and Noemi's free dance drives Danny to tears. It's achingly sentimental, every movement an extension of repressed love, and Danny buys into it fully for the length of the performance, even though he knows they're nowhere near in love with each other. They win, of course they win, and Danny snaps a blurry, too-far shot of them on the top podium, holding their medals up to their smiling faces. He finds them in the backstage area and Noemi jumps on him, squeezing him tight before demanding his medal to compare them.

Danny expects to have to make some excuses to get alone with Noah, but instead Noemi just bids them goodnight in the elevator and gets off at her floor without a fuss. He cocks an eyebrow at Noah once it's just them, and the man grimaces. "Once we're inside," is all he says.

Once the door to Noah's hotel room is shut behind them, Noah pins him to it with a deep, full-bodied kiss that makes Danny moan and clutch at him. They kiss for long minutes, until Danny is boneless, held up only by the pressure of Noah's body holding him to the door. Noah finally releases him, brushing their noses together, and sighs. "Noemi knows about us."

"You told her?" Danny asks, surprised.

Noah shakes his head. "I guess we were a little more obvious than we thought the other night. She worked it out."

"Well, she knows us both very well," Danny says, rubbing his hands up and down Noah's back in an attempt to be reassuring. "Are you okay with her knowing?"

"Does it matter now?" Noah asks, before shaking his head at himself. "I trust her, I suppose. She has as much reason as I do to keep it secret."

"And she loves us," Danny says softly. "She wouldn't do anything to hurt us."

"No," Noah agrees. "She wouldn't."

Danny bites his lip. "Out of curiosity, what reason?" Noah looks at him, confused, and he goes on, "Why didn't you want her to know?"

Noah sighs, pressing his forehead to Danny's. "Our skates,

our image, is based around the presence of romance in our performances," he says. "Our medals depend on how well we can make the judges believe in it. If word gets out that I'm gay, then that damages the judges' belief. It would feel like a betrayal, especially given how hard she's worked for the illusion of romance on her end. I can't let her down, and the fewer people who know the truth, the easier it is to keep it totally secret."

Danny runs his hands up Noah's arms to link behind his neck. "I guess that makes sense. It sucks that you have to consider it, though."

Noah smiles wryly. "It's not like you're able to be out either."

"True." There's still a worry in Noah's eyes that Danny doesn't like, so he brushes their noses together again and says, "Your free dance made me cry."

That brings the light back into Noah's face, a bashful happiness that makes Danny grin. "I was thinking of you," he confesses, voice low.

Part of Danny wants to tell him not to say things like that when they're trying to be casual about each other, but a much larger part of him wants to coo and put his tongue in Noah's mouth to get things moving, and he gladly goes with that urge instead. They stumble toward the bed, shedding clothing as they go. "Do you still want to…" Danny asks, trailing off.

Noah nods. "If you do."

"I definitely do."

Noah's fingers are long, thin but powerful, and they feel like heaven inside Danny as he takes his time prepping him. Danny urges him on with moans and words until he's gaping open and begging; only then does Noah roll a condom on and take his place between Danny's spread thighs.

Noah pushes inside him slowly, and Danny can't keep his eyes off his face. "Fuck," Noah whispers once he's fully seated, bending down to kiss him. "*Fuck*, you feel so good."

"Fuck me, Noah," Danny whines, "baby, please."

The endearment makes Noah growl like an animal and he

starts to move, little rocking thrusts at first that slowly develop into longer, deeper things that send his cock so far inside Danny he can feel it in his throat. "*Yes,*" Danny moans, ankles hooking around Noah's legs to keep him going.

Noah keeps fucking him, dropping down for kisses whenever their bodies allow, and then his face screws up, almost pained. "*Shit*, Danny, I'm not going to last," he grits out. "I can't, I—"

"It's okay," Danny says, pushing a hand into his hair. "Just give me what you can, it's alright."

Noah lasts another minute before locking his hips against Danny's with a grunting cry that almost sends Danny over the edge. "I'm sorry," he gasps once he's capable, "Danny, I'm sorry."

"Don't be sorry," Danny tells him, running his hands through his hair and holding as still as he can with a mostly-hard cock still inside him. "It's alright, I promise."

"I wanted it to be good for you," Noah says, eyes shut tight in disappointment.

Danny laughs, still petting him. "Baby, it was good for me." Noah opens his eyes and looks at him. Danny brushes a thumb over his cheek. "It's you," he says. "It's you, and so it can't not be good for me."

Noah kisses him instead of saying whatever it is he wants to say at that, and then he slides himself out of Danny's body with a wince. He locates another condom and a glove in his suitcase, pulls the glove on and rolls the condom onto Danny's still-achingly-hard cock, then slicks up two fingers and pushes them back inside, taking Danny into his mouth.

"Oh fuck, baby," Danny says, to feel that growl around his cock, "yes, yes, just like that, don't stop, *oh*…" He comes, a long slow unspooling into Noah's mouth, and collapses onto the bed with a happy sigh.

Noah takes care of their condoms and crawls back up the bed, settling against Danny's side and throwing a hand over his stomach. Danny feels him open his mouth and says, "Don't apologize again. You really don't have to."

Danny can hear the snap as Noah shuts his mouth again. "Alright," he says instead, snuggling further into Danny's shoulder. Danny sends his fingers carding through Noah's hair, his other thumb ruling over the skin of Noah's forearm where it's lying on his stomach.

It's a wrench to leave him, but he has to; they can't risk sleepovers at competitions, they agreed over the summer. Noah gazes at him sleepily as he dresses, and Danny has to lean down and kiss his forehead before he can make himself leave.

They don't get a chance to see each other again until Euros, and Danny throws himself into training the quad Lutz. He's spending more time on it now than he was during the series, with Nico's blessing, and his consistency is slowly going up. Nico agrees to let the jump into both Danny's programs the day before they leave.

Euros is, frankly, a hazy blur of sex hormones and adrenaline, and Danny doesn't remember much of it by the time it's over. He remembers landing the Lutz during his short and one-handing it during the free, earning himself a silver to Andrei's gold; he remembers sucking Andrei's cock in the rink bathroom before the gala, patting his hair back into normalcy afterward; he remembers playing footsie under the table with Noah while they have dinner with Noemi, and the fond roll of her eyes when he accidentally kicks her instead. The rest of it is a foggy cloud in his memory, but he must acquit himself well enough, because Nico doesn't say anything on the flight home, just congratulates him on his medal and puts his audiobook on.

Worlds is more of the same, although Danny has his head on a little more tightly for it. Andrei returns the favor from the Euros, giving Danny the quickest, roughest blow job he's ever had ten minutes before he has to get on the ice for the free skate. His performance components score is unusually high, inching him into the silver medal position again, and Andrei tips him a *you're welcome* wink from his place at the top of the podium.

Noah comes over the week after they get home from Tokyo and eats Danny out for forty-five minutes. Danny comes once during it, rutting his cock shamelessly against the sheets, and then Noah turns him over and slides inside him. They're both giggling as he throws Danny's legs apart and pulls his hips into his lap, and Danny can't hold back a bit of a cackle as Noah thrusts into him a half-dozen times and comes with a shout.

Noah scowls at him, but fondly, and Danny bites his lip flirtatiously as he pulls out. The mood shifts a little, though, when Noah pushes his fingers deep into Danny's hole; his eyes turn piercing, dark and intense and pinning Danny to the mattress, and instead of laughing Danny's moaning, unable to look away from his lover's face as he fingers him to another orgasm while Danny writhes and quivers under him.

Noah leaves just long enough to swirl some of Danny's mouthwash around his mouth and then comes back to where Danny is still trembling from the aftershocks. He splays himself fully on top of Danny and catches his mouth, minty-fresh tongue sweeping in like a conqueror. Danny moans again and throws his arms around him, letting himself be kissed for as long as Noah feels like it, which turns out to be quite a while.

"I'm so glad it's you," Noah mumbles sleepily, once they've stopped kissing and he's rolled off Danny to curl up against his side. "I can't picture anyone else; it could only have been you."

More non-casual talk, and once again Danny can't bring himself to protest, only wrap Noah up tighter in his arms and bury his nose in his hair. "I'm glad it's you too," he murmurs, and Noah sighs happily, already three-quarters of the way asleep.

Chapter 15

NOAH: SO GUESS what

Danny: You miss my kiss terribly and are on your way over to sweep me off my feet

Noah: Well, yes, that, minus the on my way over part, sadly

Noah: But that's not what I was talking about

Noah: You remember that crack in my ceiling?

Danny: The one over your coffee table?

Noah: Yes

Noah: Turns out it's a bigger deal than I anticipated

Noah: My contractor came by and apparently they have to replaster my whole ceiling

Noah: I need to be out of the apartment for at least three days

Danny: Omg

Danny: Yes

Noah: Silly Daniel, I haven't asked you anything yet

Danny: Ask, then

Noah: Can I stay at yours for a few days next week?

Danny: YES

Danny: We'll play house

Danny: Domesticity galore

Noah: Thank you

Noah: That sounds lovely

Noah: I can't wait

Danny: Me neither

Noah comes on a Friday. He's scheduled the plasterers to come and do their work over days neither of them have to skate very much, so he and Danny can have the most time together. Danny lets him in with a smile, standing aside as Noah comes in and drops his suitcase on the floor, then reaches for him, sweeping him into his arms with a deep kiss. "Hi, honey," he murmurs, eyes bright with amusement. "I'm home."

Danny presses their mouths together again, a sweet, lingering tease of a kiss, then pulls back. "Are you hungry?"

Noah's arms tighten around him. "Not for food."

Danny rolls his eyes, biting back a smile. "Then let's get your suitcase into the bedroom," he says, looking up through his eyelashes at Noah, who's staring down at him hungrily. Danny takes his hand and picks up the suitcase with the other, giving him another coquettish look before dragging him into the bedroom.

They make love as desperately as if they hadn't seen each other just last week, Noah's thighs tight around Danny's hips as Danny thrusts frantically into him, their mouths panting against each other. When it's over, Noah confesses to an actual hunger, for food rather than cock. Danny dresses himself in his sluttiest bathrobe and throws some chicken and vegetables in the oven, and they make out lazily against the counter while the smell of dinner permeates the kitchen. Noah feathers kisses all over his face and neck and shoulders, and Danny clings to him, letting the soft sounds that start in his chest out and trying to quell the ferocious pounding of his heart.

The next morning, Danny wakes on his stomach with Noah sprawled across his back. Smiling privately, he frees himself from

Noah's grip and heads into the kitchen, putting a pot of coffee on and turning on the faucet to wash the dishes from dinner. He's only a few minutes into it, rinsing the soap suds from a plate, when arms wrap around him from behind and Noah's cheek, a little stubbly, presses against his own. "Good morning," Danny murmurs, nuzzling him.

In answer, Noah kisses his cheek, and then his jaw, and then just behind his ear. Danny is wearing a low-slung pair of sweatpants and nothing else, and Noah's hands start to roam, stroking over his stomach and thumbing his nipples while he licks and nips at Danny's jawline. Danny moans, letting his eyes fall shut and his head tip to one side, his cock starting to swell.

One of Noah's hands dips low, venturing under his waistband to brush against his cock before taking him firmly in hand. Danny whines, and Noah starts sucking lightly on his neck while he strokes. It's a dry grip, and the friction is just right. Danny wraps one hand around Noah's moving wrist, the other propping himself up against the counter.

He's vocal in his appreciation, moaning and gasping and pushing his ass back to grind into Noah's crotch. Noah hums and Danny can feel the vibration in his lips against the tender skin of his neck, where Noah is still latched on. His hand never stops, stroking Danny in the way he's come to know Danny loves. The coffee machine finishes at some point before Danny does, the air filling with the familiar aroma. It combines with the smell of Noah, still sleep-warm and sharpened by his arousal, and Danny lets his head loll back on his neck in delight.

Noah catches Danny's come in his hand when he spills and shudders, pulling off his neck with a gorgeous wet pop. "What was that for?" Danny murmurs, leaning against him while he catches his breath.

Noah kisses his cheek again, reaching for the roll of paper towels next to the sink. "Just feeling lucky this morning," he murmurs, tearing a sheet off. "The coffee's ready." With that he's gone, leaving Danny to collect himself and finish the dishes.

Noah stays the whole weekend. He has to skate on Saturday and Danny has a workout Sunday that he can't skip, but otherwise they spend the time holed up in Danny's apartment, wrapped around each other while watching TV or abandoning all pretense to fuck on every surface they can make work. It's more sex than Danny has had packed into a concentrated span of time since the Olympics and Vardan, and he's never felt more alive, invigorated by every touch of Noah's hand or cock or tongue.

In between the rampant fucking, there's talking, Danny's head in Noah's lap with fingers carding through his hair, or over a meal at Danny's tiny kitchen table. Danny tells Noah about his plans for the season, and Noah tells Danny about his family. Danny learns Noah's favorite color, blue, which has somehow never come up before, and they both agree that cats are the ideal domestic animal. "Good to know we agree," Noah says, trailing a finger against Danny's cheek; Danny's other is pressed against his stomach.

"Good to know," Danny echoes, and catches the finger in between his lips.

Noah leaves on Monday afternoon, when the smell of fresh paint has dissipated from his apartment. "Thanks for letting me stay," he says, pulling Danny into his arms again before he goes. "We'll have to do this again. I had a lovely time."

"Me too," Danny says, copping one last feel of Noah's ass. "You're welcome anytime."

Noah's dedicated attention at the kitchen sink left a mark on Danny's neck, but it's mostly faded by the time Danny has to report back to the rink, and if Nico notices, he doesn't let on. Danny is landing the quad Lutz more than eighty percent of the time now, and they're building his programs for the upcoming season around it.

The programs are set by early August. His short program is a jive, fast and high-spirited, and his free skate is a slow, sexy prowl of a dance, thrumming bass and a clinging costume that leaves very little to the imagination.

Noemi brings up the elephant in the room a week after his birthday, at a lunch that's just her and Danny, eating Chinese food out of the containers in her tiny studio. "I haven't wanted to pry," she says through a mouthful of rice and chicken, "and if I figured if you didn't bring it up, things must be going okay. But are they? With Noah, I mean. Is he treating you alright?"

Danny blushes despite himself, and Noemi raises an eyebrow. "He's treating me just fine," he says. "Wonderfully," he adds, flushing deeper. Noemi somehow manages to roll her eyes and smile encouragingly at the same time. "It's really good, Noe. You don't have to worry."

"I remember how he disappeared on you after you kissed him," Noemi says. "I'll always worry about you, Danny; you're my best friend. But are things getting properly serious with him? He stayed with you for a few days, right?"

Danny sobers, stabbing his chopsticks into his own beef and broccoli. "I want things to be serious with him," he confesses, and she frowns. "And I think he wants that too. So sometimes we sort of slip into it. But for the most part we're just casual, like we agreed."

"Okay," she says slowly. "As long as you're happy."

"I'm very happy," he confirms, and it's true. He and Noah aren't as committed as he dreams of, but they have a good time together, and he knows Noah cares about him too.

She nods decisively. "And if that ever changes, I'll kill him." Danny laughs and the mood is broken.

One evening in early September, his plans with Noah are abruptly canceled by the onset of a sudden head cold. "I'm sorry," Noah says stuffily over the phone. "I don't want to risk you getting sick."

"It's alright," Danny says. "Do you need soup? I can bring you soup."

Noah laughs nasally. "Maybe tomorrow? Right now I just want to sleep."

"Take care of yourself," Danny tells him firmly, and once Noah promises, they hang up. Faced with a sudden evening alone, Danny decides to doll himself up and take himself out. There's a gay club nearby he hasn't been to in a while, and he could do with some non-skating-related dancing. It's still relatively quiet when he gets there, and he installs himself at the bar with a drink to wait for the crowd to thicken out a bit on the dance floor. He's just wishing he'd thought to bring a book when someone leans onto the counter next to him.

When he looks, it's a short, lean man with thin pink and blue glasses and a mop of dishwater hair. "Hi," he says in broad, flat English. "Sorry to interrupt your evening. It's just, a few years ago, I promised myself that if I ever had the chance I'd shoot my shot with you, and here you are, and here I am, so to honor my past self's promise, I figured I had to at least come over and say hello. Can I buy you a drink?"

Danny lets the torrent of quickly-spoken words wash over him and takes the man in. He looks nervous, with a quirky little smile and fingers tap-tap-tapping against the bar, but he's got a brave look on his face too, and Danny really, really likes bravery. "Only if you have one with me," he says, his best smile spreading across his face. "Have a seat; stay awhile."

"Great," the man says, grinning back widely. He drops into the chair next to Danny's, signaling to the bartender and ordering another whiskey for Danny and a martini for himself. "I hope it doesn't freak you out that I know who you are," he says, turning back to Danny. "I promise not to tell anyone you were here."

"I appreciate that," Danny says. It's the first rule of a gay bar, after all. "What's your name?"

"Nat," he says. "I'm here on business."

"From America?"

"Yes." Nat accepts his martini from the bartender and takes a sip. "Business meeting with the Swiss offices, of course Skype wouldn't suffice, so I had to come in person."

"Lucky me," Danny drawls.

Nat flushes a delightful deep red but pushes on. "What brings you out tonight, Mr. Schaer? Danny? What do you like to be called?"

"Danny is perfect," Danny says. "And I'm here because my plans for the evening got canceled and I didn't want to sit at home all night."

"No plans, huh?" Nat gives him a bold once-over that makes it abundantly clear that he thinks that's the best news he's heard all night. Danny winks at him, charmed, and he goes that delicious red again. "What about in the morning?"

"I have to be at the rink at nine," Danny says, leaning back in his chair. "So I should warn you, if you're a serial killer, I will be missed."

Nat laughs, a thin, reedy thing that nonetheless makes Danny smile. "Oh, I don't want to kill you, Danny," he says. Danny sees his eyes twinkle behind his glasses.

Danny looks him up and down, blatantly lascivious to see if he can get him to blush a third time. "Oh? What do you want to do to me instead?"

Nat's jaw drops momentarily, a look of happy shock spreading across his face. He masters himself quickly, though, and leans in to say, "My company's put me up in an apartment a block away, if you'd like to find out."

Danny grins, triumph warming his belly. "Lead the way, good sir."

Instead of getting up, though, Nat makes a face. "Look," he says. "Judging by the fact that you're in what Google assured me was Bern's biggest gay bar, and the fact that you've just agreed to go home with me, I assume you like men." He holds up a hand. "I won't tell anyone or out you to anyone, I promise."

Danny shrugs. "Assume away, then."

Nat takes a deep breath, then looks him square in the eye. "How do you feel about clitorises?"

"Oh." Danny takes a second to consider how to phrase it. "No experience. Very willing."

"I can work with that," Nat says. "Let's go."

Danny signals for his bill.

Chapter 16

NAT ALL BUT drags him out of the bar by the hand, dropping it once they're outside. "What do you do?" Danny asks on the walk to his lodgings.

"I'm Chief Financial Officer of a small company," Nat says. "We make apps."

"Impressive." Danny gives him a glowing glance and he winks.

There isn't much time for conversation, though, because Nat's apartment really is only a block away from the club. Danny relinks their hands in the elevator, for the hell of it; Nat squeezes his fingers and smiles.

Nat fumbles with the still-unfamiliar keys at the door; Danny helps by sliding his hand slowly along Nat's hip to rest on the small of his back. Nat thumps his forehead into the door endearingly, and then opens it. Onto a very, *very* nice apartment.

"Wow," Danny says, stepping in to let the other man shut the door behind them. "Your company must really love you."

"Startups," Nat says, dropping the keys into a bowl by the door. "There are a lot of downsides, but there are some *very* good upsides, too."

Danny gives him a sidelong grin, all canines and hunger. "Hoo boy," Nat says. "Okay, rules, but first I have to kiss you, after that look. Incoming." He walks forward and Danny pulls him the last few steps, putting his hand to his neck to sweep him into a deep, consuming kiss. Nat whimpers against his mouth and puts his hands on Danny's shoulders. "Rules," he says, taking a deep breath. "Are you okay with rules?"

Danny has to shut his eyes against the shudder that goes

through him. "I think I love rules," he admits, grinning wryly.

"Right, okay," Nat says, voice very high. "Fuck, that was hot. Okay, rules. One, I know what I called it back in the bar, but it's my cock and will be referred to as such. Got it?"

"Got it," Danny confirms.

"Two, I want you inside me, if you're game, but you're coming in the back door, not the front." Nat's eyes are flickering from Danny's eyes to his mouth and back again. Danny licks his lips and Nat swears again under his breath. "Three, top surgery took basically all the feeling in my nipples, so don't waste your time."

"Understood," Danny says. "I'm game for anything, but can I suck your cock first?"

"You want to?" Nat looks as surprised as he can while still looking incredibly turned on.

Danny nods. "I like the idea of being on my knees for you," he murmurs.

"Fuck," Nat intones on a long breath, before leaning up and taking Danny's mouth again.

Nat is an *enthusiastic* kisser, all suction and tongue and moans, enough to get Danny half-hard in his jeans before anyone even touches his shirt buttons. Nat gets to them quickly enough, though, and before long Danny is shrugging out of his shirt, letting it fall to the floor. Nat takes a step back to take him in.

"Mmph," he grunts, hand sliding down from Danny's shoulder to shamelessly grope his right pectoral. "Holy God, you *are* an athlete, aren't you?" Danny laughs, earning a helpless giggle from Nat. "Wow. Okay. I promise not to objectify you all night."

"Hey, it's a lot of work, keeping this body," Danny says. "It's nice for it to be appreciated. Any clothes you're willing to lose in exchange?"

Nat reaches behind his head to grab hold of his shirt, pulling it off in one fell swoop. He's in reasonably good shape himself, a toned, firm chest and the faint outline of abs. There are two thin scars on his chest, one under each nipple. Danny kisses him again, pulling their torsos together, both of them moaning on impact. He puts a hand flat on Nat's stomach, pulling another groan from the man, and starts to slip it ever-so-slowly downward.

Nat doesn't stop him; instead, he moves his kisses to Danny's jaw and unbuckles his own jeans, letting the front gape open. Danny hums appreciatively and continues his descent, his fingers reaching the tight curls of Nat's pubic hair.

"No touching the front door," Nat reminds him breathlessly, before biting into the soft skin under his chin.

"I won't," Danny says. "Just…ringing the doorbell."

Nat lets out a shocked, delighted laugh that devolves into a harsh sigh as Danny's middle finger reaches his cock. "Light circles," Nat instructs on a breath. "*Oh*, yes, just like that." He kisses Danny again, breath hitching on throaty exhalations as Danny carefully touches him. His hips are thrusting shallowly into Danny's hand, and though Danny isn't touching any further back, wetness reaches his fingers, making the glide slippery and smooth. "Fuck, you've got good hands," Nat whispers against Danny's lips. "Gonna make me come."

"What do you need?" Danny asks.

Nat shakes his head, hips moving a little faster. "Just don't stop." So Danny doesn't, circling and brushing his cock until Nat's head tips back and he cries out, his pelvis coming down onto Danny's hand again and again.

Danny rides him through it, fascinated by how long it takes for Nat's shakes to subside and his head to come back up. "Well done," Nat murmurs, throwing his arms around Danny's neck for another kiss. He takes Danny's wrist and pulls his hand out of his trousers, bringing his fingers to his mouth and starting to suck them. Once they're clean, he uses his hold on Danny's wrist to pull him toward the bedroom.

"Still want to go down on me?" Nat asks, shimmying out of his jeans. Danny takes that as his cue and follows suit, tossing his own jeans and briefs aside and smirking at the way Nat licks his lips at the sight of his cock. "I've got at least two more orgasms in me tonight."

"Sounds perfect," Danny says. "Do you have dams?"

There's a suitcase in the corner of the bedroom. Nat roots around in it for a minute, bare ass temptingly in the air, before emerging victorious, a dental dam, a condom, and a nitrile glove in hand. "Knew I still had stuff in here." He tosses the dam to Danny and drops the condom and glove on the bed before draping himself across it. "Come here."

They kiss for long, hungry minutes, the lines of their naked bodies pressing together. Nat gets a hand in Danny's hair and a hand on his ass and devours him, thighs bracketing his hips. Danny breaks away from his mouth to move up to his ear and then down his neck; Nat tips his head to the other side and lets out a constant stream of appreciative noises.

As per the rules, Danny bypasses Nat's nipples when he gets to them. He does give one scar a long lick, and Nat jolts under him. "Good or bad?" Danny asks, looking up.

"Mmm, neutral to good," is the answer, so Danny does it again before moving on, kissing his way down Nat's abs and across his hips until he can get his teeth into Nat's thigh. Nat moans encouragingly, so Danny leaves a decent mark on the meat of it before opening the dam and settling it into place.

"Fuck," Nat says almost conversationally as Danny licks across his cock. "Fuck, yes, keep licking for now, oh shit, yes yes *yes*..." His hips flex as Danny obeys, pushing his cock that much harder into Danny's tongue. Danny sets up a rhythm before too long, long licks with the flat of his tongue and then careful flicks with the tip. Nat props himself up on his elbows, head hanging back, and chants a litany of praise. "Fuck, suck me," he says finally, gasping. "Suck my cock, Danny, do it." Danny takes Nat's cock between his lips and sucks on it, still flicking it with his tongue, and after a minute of that Nat cries out and starts to shake again, nearly getting Danny in the nose with his pubic bone as he thrusts up into Danny's mouth.

Nat collapses onto the bed once the orgasm is through with him, breathing heavily. Danny peels the dam away from his skin and walks it over to the trash can, and then comes back to the bed and plasters himself to Nat. Nat kisses him between pants, curling both hands into Danny's hair and tugging. Danny is rock hard but surprisingly calm about it. "I think I could just keep making you come all night and be satisfied," he says into Nat's cheek.

Nat laughs. "Don't worry, big boy, you'll get yours," he says, patting Danny absently on the shoulder. "Just give me a minute and I'll start opening myself up for you."

"I could do it," Danny suggests, trying not to sound too eager.

Nat squints one eye open and looks at him. "You're doing an awful lot for me tonight," he says, mock-suspicious.

Danny shrugs. "It's fun."

Nat grins. "Well, alright then. To work, Mr. Schaer."

"You're one up on me," Danny says, reaching for the glove and pulling it on. There's lube in the nightstand and he grabs the bottle, pouring some into his hands. "What's your last name?"

"Bell," Nat says. He hooks his hand under his thighs and splays himself open, a gorgeous, wet display that makes Danny have to swear a little under his breath before reaching for him. "Nice and boring."

"I like it," Danny says, circling one lubed, gloved finger around Nat's back door. "It's not boring at all. Bells are musical."

"Are you saying I'm musical?"

Danny winks at him. "I'm certainly playing you like an instrument," he drawls, pushing the tip of his finger inside.

"*Fuck!* Okay, well played," Nat grits out. "In both the instrumental and the comedic timing sense. Deeper." Danny slides in deeper and Nat groans, biting his lip. Danny rolls his finger around, pulling at Nat's rim and enjoying the almost pained sounds coming from the man's throat. "Two now," Nat says after a few minutes, and Danny obediently lubes up another finger and sends them both inside, stretching carefully.

By the time Danny has three fingers buried inside him, Nat's fucking back as best he can from his back. "I feel like a turtle on its shell," he grumbles, and Danny barks a laugh and kisses the mark on his thigh. "Let me see that piece again?" Danny displays himself proudly. "One, gorgeous, and two, I'm ready for you," Nat says. "Let's get that in me."

"How do you want me?" Danny asks, slipping his fingers free and stripping the glove off. He drops it onto the floor and reaches for the condom.

Nat rolls onto his hands and knees. "Like this?"

"Your wish is my command." Danny rubs lube over his sheathed cock and kneels his way over to Nat. "Can I spank you?" It's not an urge he's ever really felt before, but something about Nat's pert ass waving at him makes him want to leave another mark.

"Mmm, go for it," Nat says over his shoulder, wiggling more at him. Danny smacks him, leaving a bright pink handprint on each cheek, and then lines himself up and starts pushing home.

True to form, Nat swears and lets his head hang down as Danny slides inside him. "God that's good," he gasps, dropping down to his elbows. Danny comes to rest balls-deep and runs his hands over Nat's back and sides, biting his lip against his own curses.

"Hold still," Nat orders him, and starts sliding forward, reversing course halfway to slap his ass against Danny's hips and take him in again. They both cry out, Danny's hands tightening on his hips, and Nat does it again and again, until Danny can't help snapping forward to meet his backward thrusts.

Danny loses track of time a little, lost in the way sweat is beading on Nat's pale, freckly back, until Nat grunts and says, "Fuck, I'm getting close."

Danny bends at the waist, pounding into him faster and harder. "I'm close too," he manages; his balls are tight and his stomach is twisting in that familiar way that means he's about to tip over.

"You first," Nat pants over his shoulder, so Danny lets go, slamming into him with a few more broken thrusts before his cock pulses and he has to tip his head back and cry out. In front of him, Nat balances on one elbow, the other hand disappearing between his legs, and then he's crying out too, his asshole convulsing around Danny's cock in a way that milks a few more drops out of him.

Danny pulls himself free and flops down next to where Nat is already flat on his stomach. "Did I live up to your fantasies?" he asks cheekily as they catch their breath.

"A plus," Nat murmurs, grinning. "Teenage dream fulfilled."

"Good, good."

They lie there for a few more minutes before Danny feels up to standing and dressing. Nat rolls onto his side and watches him pull his briefs and jeans on. "I think your shirt's in the living room," he adds helpfully when Danny starts looking around for it.

"I think you're right." Danny pads out and finds it puddled on the carpet. Nat follows him, still gloriously bare, and wraps his arms around Danny's neck once the shirt is on. Danny gives him a thorough kissing goodbye, stealing one last palmful of Nat's ass while their mouths work together. "This was fun," he says when they finally pull apart.

"Very fun," Nat agrees. "You've given me an evening I… can never tell anyone about," he finishes, eyes widening with the realization.

Danny laughs. "I won't be closeted forever. Once I'm out, you can brag to your heart's content, if you like."

"No pressure," Nat says hastily. "I can totally keep schtum for the rest of my life; I was just teasing."

"Eh." Danny shrugs. "None felt, but also I don't really want to be closeted the rest of my life. Probably just the rest of my competitive career."

"Totally fair." Nat kisses him again and lets him go. "I'll put money on you over Lebed this season," he says. Danny winks at him, pleased, and leaves with a skip in his step.

Chapter 17

WITH THE QUAD Lutz now firmly in his repertoire, Danny breezes through the Grand Prix series with an ease that surprises him. It helps that he doesn't have to compete directly with Andrei in his two assignments, but the other skater doesn't seem surprised. "The old guard is moving out," Andrei says on the phone one night in early December, "and we've always been at the top of the class for our generation. I picked you as my foil for a reason, Danny."

"And that reason is that I'll always be half a step behind you?" Danny asks, grumpy from a long day of practice before the Final, and sore from a couple of missed Lutzes that sent him slamming into the ice.

"Because you're the only real competition I have," Andrei says, not a hint of arrogance in his tone despite his words.

"Whoa there, tiger," Danny says, flopping onto his couch with an ice pack. "You've won one season. Lots of people have done that."

"No one else has won as many seasons as I'm going to," Andrei tells him, still matter-of-fact rather than boastful. "Last season was just the start."

"I'm a little offended you don't actually seem to view me as competition, despite your pretty words," Danny says, a little stung.

"Don't be stupid," Andrei says. "Of course you are. I'm not explaining this right." He goes silent for a moment, and Danny lets him be, settling the ice pack on the worst of the bruising on his right hip. "I'm going to do great things in this sport," Andrei says finally. "I already have, and I'm going to do more. But I couldn't do any of it if I didn't have you on the podium beside me. I need you, Danny, and what's more, you need me. We're a matched pair on the ice."

"Well, I have no doubt about the great things you'll do," Danny says, appeased. "But that doesn't mean I'm just going to let you win every season. I'll give you a fight every time, and I'm going to win some."

"I know you'll fight, Danny." Andrei's voice is warm. "That's why I…" He falters, and Danny has to smile.

"Say it, Red Swan," he says teasingly. "Say that's why you love me."

Andrei groans. "You're insufferable." He goes a little quiet again. "I think you're my best friend."

"Say that again, and don't sound nauseous this time," Danny says, amused.

"Shut up and say it back," Andrei snaps.

"I love you too, and you're one of my best friends too," Danny tells him indulgently. "I don't mind being your matched pair, Andrei, really I don't; I just mind the assumption that I'll always be the one losing."

"It isn't losing," Andrei says. "It's winning silver."

"When did you get so well-adjusted?"

"Insufferable," Andrei mutters again, and Danny laughs.

Quebec is bitingly cold in December, even for someone as resolutely Swiss as Danny, and he, Noah, and Noemi are like a walking scarf commercial as they make their way toward the nearest restaurant for dinner the night they all arrive for the Final. "Remind me why we do a winter sport?" Noemi gripes, unwinding her two scarves from around her neck once they're inside.

"The cold makes our cheeks flush winningly," Danny tells her, shrugging out of his coat to hang it on the peg by the table. "I'm starving."

They settle in, Noah next to Danny and Noemi across from them, and peruse the menu. Danny hooks his foot around Noah's ankle for the hell of it, and has to bite back a grin when

Noah's foot nuzzles back. Noemi sends them a glowing, exasperated look; Danny puts on his most innocent expression and grins to himself when it makes her laugh.

They've just ordered when Danny catches sight of a familiar flash of red coming in the door of the restaurant. "Andrei!" he calls, waving. Andrei looks over at him, says something to the host, and makes his way over to their table.

"Danny," he says with a nod of greeting. "And the top ice dancers of Switzerland," he adds, eyes flicking to Noah and Noemi. "Are you hosting your own Nationals?"

"Ugh, don't remind us," Danny says with a wince. Nationals overlaps with the Final this year; it wasn't a difficult decision, but missing Nationals is still a wrench. "What are you doing here?"

"Getting food," Andrei says, raising an eyebrow at him.

"Don't be cute," Danny snarks back. "Want to join us?"

Andrei's eyes flick to Noemi, and then to Noah, who has gone very still, Danny's foot still hooked around his ankle. "I can't," he says. "Fyodor and I are wining and dining a sponsor tonight. But thank you for the invitation."

"Can't lose that sponsor money," Noemi agrees. "Another time."

"Sure," Andrei says. "Danny, I'll see you later?"

There's a strange sort of pointedness to his tone, and a sharpness in his eyes that Danny doesn't usually see outside of the bedroom. "Of course," Danny says, and Andrei gives them a little wave and goes back to the host, who shows him to a table across the restaurant.

"I've never actually spoken to him before," Noemi says in a hushed voice, leaning over the table. "I'm a little starstruck."

"Don't be," Danny tells her. "He's not that special." She titters, and their conversation resumes, although Noah is a little quieter than usual.

Andrei, shockingly, one-hands a triple Lutz during the short programs, so Danny ends the day in a rare first. Nico drags him schmoozing and interviewing for a bit, then releases him. "Go to bed," he says warningly. "You have a lead. We don't want you losing it because you were distracted and up all night."

"Yes, Coach," Danny says. Nico claps him on the arm, and he heads back to the hotel.

It's late, but if he squints at the time he can justify another half an hour before bed, so he wanders up to Noah's room and knocks on the door. "Oh," Noah says, opening it in his pajamas. "I didn't expect to see you tonight."

"I only have a few minutes, but I wanted to see you," Danny says. "Can I come in?"

Noah lets him in and kisses him, sweet and quick. "You skated well today," he says, climbing back into bed. Danny crawls on top of the covers and insinuates himself into Noah's arms. "A well-deserved small gold."

"You did, too," Danny says. He and Noemi are in a neck-and-neck second place going into their free dance in two days. "Are you nervous?"

Noah shakes his head. "I'm rarely nervous once I'm actually at the competition," he says. "It's the lead-up that gets me." Danny hums in acknowledgment and snuggles in closer, one finger tracing meaningless patterns across Noah's sleep shirt. "How long have you been sleeping with Andrei Lebed?" Noah asks abruptly, after a few minutes.

Danny blinks, startled. "Who says I'm sleeping with him?"

"He made it pretty evident at dinner the other day," Noah says darkly.

Danny sighs. "Don't ask me questions that require outing other people, Noah. I don't do that. You know I'm sleeping with other people, but I won't be specific if they're not out."

Noah lets out a long breath. "No, you're right. That wasn't fair. I'm sorry."

He's still a little stiff, and Danny props his chin on his shoulder, amused. "Are you experiencing the emotion known as jealousy?"

"No," Noah says instantly, and then, "Yes. A little." He groans, rubbing his face with one hand.

Danny laughs and kisses his cheek. "It's a good look on

you," he tells him.

"Is it?"

Danny nods. "I like a little possession in my lover, as long as it doesn't get unhealthy."

"Good to know," Noah murmurs. "It doesn't feel good."

Danny sits up, catching Noah's chin and turning him to face him. "I know it's been a long time since we talked about what we are to each other," he says. "But this seems like a good time to remind you that anytime you want to be exclusive, we can do that. All you have to do is ask."

Noah looks at him for a long moment, then sighs. "I don't think that's a good idea right now," he says, voice low. "Much as I wish it were different."

"That's okay," Danny says. "I don't want to push you where you're not comfortable. What we have is good; I'm not saying it isn't. But I don't know how much longer I'm willing to pretend that we only feel casually about each other."

Noah grimaces apologetically. "That's fair." He takes Danny's hand, rubbing his thumb over the back of it while he thinks. "I don't want to sit here and tell you that my feelings for you aren't serious," he says, "because they are. But I'm not in a position to be a good boyfriend right now. You deserve better than what I could give you if we tried this seriously."

Danny turns his hand over in Noah's, lacing their fingers together and trying to quell the nervous beating of his heart. "Alright," he says. "Like I said, I don't want to push you. What we've been doing is great. For the time being."

"Thank you," Noah says, gratitude laced through his voice. Danny kisses him and Noah melts into it, letting go of Danny's hand to cradle his jaw and tilt his head for better access.

They kiss for a few minutes before he pulls away and smiles. "I'm proud of us," he says.

Noah smiles back at him, stroking his cheek. "Mature, healthy check-ins," he says. "Who knew?" Danny grins and steals a final kiss before taking his leave.

Danny manages a good night's sleep once he finally makes it back to his room, waking with enough time before official practice to obtain coffee and bagels and drop one of each off at Nico's room. "You're peppy," his coach says, rubbing his face and drinking deep.

"Slept well," Danny says. "I feel ready for today."

"Good," Nico says. "Eat your breakfast. I'll meet you at the rink." He shuts his door.

Andrei finds him while the ladies are doing their free skates and the men are warming up. "I hope I didn't make things awkward for you with Favre," he says, pulling Danny aside. "He seemed a little tense when we ran into each other the other night."

Danny sighs, rubbing the bridge of his nose. "I really wish people would stop asking me things that rely on me potentially outing others," he says pointedly, and Andrei has the grace to look abashed. "Without revealing anything that isn't mine to reveal," Danny goes on, "he and I are fine. No awkwardness at all."

Andrei nods. "I don't want to get in the way of a proper love affair. Not that you and Favre are having one," he adds at Danny's glare. "Just, if you were."

"If we were," Danny says, "it wouldn't really be your place to get possessive over me." However hot Danny found it in the moment.

"I know," Andrei says, "and I won't, I promise. I'm not used to sharing your attention, but I will get good at it."

"I have every faith in you." Danny claps him on the shoulder. "Now can I please finish warming up?"

"Right," Andrei says. "Carry on. I want a proper fight from you."

Danny gives him one, gives him all he's got, but Andrei's free skate this season is a thing of pure beauty, and Danny can't even feel bitter over taking silver to him. "Well skated," he says to Andrei on the podium.

The look Andrei gives him is a little more heated than they usually get in public, and Danny tells him off for it in Andrei's hotel room that night, one hand twisted tight in his hair as he fucks his thighs. Danny thinks he gets the message well enough.

Chapter 18

DANNY SCROLLS THROUGH his shiny new Instagram account, liking all the pictures from Nationals with a bittersweet sigh.

Nico looks at his phone screen and puts a hand on Danny's shoulder. "Look at it this way," he says. "You gave someone a chance at gold that they wouldn't have had if you'd been there."

"Thanks," Danny says, considering this. "That helps, I think."

"Win it back next year," Nico tells him. "For now, break's over. Time to focus on the Euros."

Danny spends the month and a half between the Final and the Euros working hard enough that he barely sees Noah, let alone Noemi. They make do with late-night phone calls while icing and the scattered meme sent on breaks during the day.

Noah: I want to see you at the Euros

Noah: I miss you

Danny: I know, I miss you too

Danny: I've been studying the schedule

Danny: Friday night, maybe? You'll be done

Noah: If it won't distract you

Danny: I'll be fine

Noah: I'll pencil you in, then

Danny: :-*

They land in Sheffield, England, on a Tuesday in late January.

"God, I hate England," Nico gripes as they run from the cab into the hotel as quickly as possible.

"I'll win and make it worth your while," Danny promises.

"You'd better."

He wants to track Andrei down—the other skater hasn't been holding his end of their text conversation up lately—but he can't find him anywhere, so he spends the evening in Noemi's room with her and Noah, comparing the base technical scores of all their competitors and calculating their odds of winning. "You guys have got this in the bag," Danny tells them. "I, on the other hand, may be fucked."

"Nonsense," Noemi says grandly, crossing her feet where they sit on his back. "You nearly had Lebed at the Final; you can beat him now." When Danny doesn't respond, she adds, "Noah, say something encouraging."

"Uh," Noah says. Danny starts to cackle at the caught-out look on his face. "Uhhh…"

"Seriously?" Noemi demands as Danny bursts into proper laughter. "This is your lover, and you can't think of anything to say?"

"Sorry," Noah says. "I never said I was good at emotional support."

Danny gets ahold of himself. "No, but you're very pretty, and that makes up for it," he says, one last snicker bursting forth.

"Well, at least I've got that going for me," Noah murmurs, but he winks when Danny catches his eye.

The short dance is right after the opening ceremonies the next day, and Danny does well enough in the morning public practice that Nico lets him go without a fight. Noah and Noemi are far and away the best of the lot, and half the audience give them a standing ovation when they take their bows. Danny hollers through his cupped hands loud enough that Noemi looks over at him and blows him a kiss when they skate off the ice.

Andrei finally makes an appearance at warm-ups before the men's short the next day. "There you are," Danny says, taking a break to walk over to where he's stretching his triceps. "You've been off the grid for a month."

"Sorry," Andrei says, grimacing. "Been busy training; not a lot of time for socializing."

"I've been busy training too," Danny tells him pointedly, "but I still made time for my friends."

Andrei grimaces again. "I said I'm sorry. I'll do better. It's just, there's a lot of pressure on me."

Danny relents, patting him on the shoulder. "Heavy is the head that wears the crown."

"Something like that," Andrei agrees.

Random order means Andrei skates before Danny, so Danny doesn't see his short program. He hears the crowd, though, and their cheers bear out the score that's read out for him. Nico, never far, puts a hand on his shoulder. "Don't try to beat him," he says. "Try to beat your best performance."

Danny nods, takes a swallow of water, and starts jogging up and down the hallway.

He ends the day in the spot that is starting to become all too familiar: second to Andrei's first. "Well skated," Andrei tells him as they're packing up for the night.

"You too," Danny says. "You'll be tough to beat."

"That's the idea," Andrei says with a wink.

Noah and Noemi clean up the next day, as expected. Nico has Danny in a rink across town during their free dance, so he can't see it live, but he watches the recording on YouTube while Noah takes a shower afterward. "Is it weird that I find your twizzles pretty sexy?" Danny asks when he comes out, toweling his hair with a tempting vein of water still dripping down his chest.

"Yes," Noah says. "Twizzles aren't sexy."

"They are when you do them."

Noah gives him a glowing look, tossing his hair towel aside and undoing the one around his waist, leaving him devastatingly bare and glistening. He comes forward slowly, lowering himself to the bed and crawling until he's fully on top of Danny, leaning down to press their mouths together with a heat that makes

Danny moan and push closer.

"How do you want me?" Danny breathes into his mouth, one hand pushed into his wet, thick, gorgeous hair.

Noah licks across Danny's lower lip. "Inside me," he says. "Inside me and under me."

They get Danny out of his clothes in record time, and Noah passes him the lube and a condom. "I started in the shower," he says, so Danny pushes two fingers into him, eyes flickering shut at the tight, grasping heat. He knows where Noah's prostate is by now and he brushes against it, making Noah gasp and clench even tighter around him.

Noah slips down onto his cock with a low, drawn-out groan that makes Danny swear and clutch at his hips. "God," Noah breathes, head tossed back to reveal the long, corded column of his neck. "I could fuck myself on your cock for the rest of my life and never have enough."

Danny strokes his thigh as he settles into his lap. "I would happily fuck you every day for the rest of our lives," he says, breath coming harshly, "except I would miss *your* cock inside *me*."

Noah grins down at him and rests his weight on Danny's chest. "Who says we can't do both?" he asks, a wicked tilt to his lips. He rocks his hips forward and then rolls them back, and both of them groan. "I'll fuck you in the morning," he goes on, doing it again, "and you'll fuck me at night."

"With—oh *fuck*, Noah—with blow jobs for lunch?" Danny says with a laugh, lifting his hips to fuck into Noah as Noah slips back onto him. "And I'd need, *yes*, I'd need to eat you out a few times a week on top of that."

Noah moans, picking up the pace. His cock is dragging along Danny's stomach, and he ruts harder against him. "We'd have to schedule everything else around sex," he pants, moving his hands to the sheets on either side of Danny's head for more leverage. "Skating, responsibilities, everything would have to take a backseat to our fuck schedule."

Danny grits his teeth and shoves his torso up, slamming his

mouth into Noah's in a kiss that knocks their teeth together in a way that would be painful if he could feel pain at the moment. "Fuck it," he murmurs, "let it all burn, as long as we make each other feel this good."

"Fuck, Danny," Noah whimpers, eyes screwing shut. "*Fuck me.*"

And Danny does, one hand propping himself up while the other grips Noah's hip to hold him in place and drag him down to meet Danny's thrusts. He fucks him and fucks him and fucks him until Noah comes untouched with a little scream and Danny slams into his clenching hole and follows him over the edge.

Noah collapses onto his chest once he's unseated himself, and they catch their breath, cuddling. "One day we're going to have bad sex," Danny muses idly, fingers stroking through Noah's hair.

Noah snickers. "Seems unlikely from my vantage point."

"Statistically, I mean," Danny says. "It can't all be mind-bogglingly amazing."

Noah looks up at him. "Danny, every time I top, it's over in under five minutes," he says drily. "That's not mind-bogglingly amazing."

"Yes it is," Danny insists. "You're a good top, and I always have a great time. We just need to get you a cockring, or some numbing gel. Not because you need to last longer," he adds hastily at the look in Noah's eye. "Just because it bothers you, and I don't want you worrying about it when you could be having joyous sex with me."

Noah sighs and puts his cheek back on Danny's shoulder. "I'll look into it," he mumbles sleepily. "Wake me in twenty minutes."

Naturally, Danny's asleep in ten, and they both wake to the buzzing of his alarm at dawn. "Ugh," Danny says eloquently, poking it silent. "Good morning," he tells the top of Noah's head.

Noah sits up and stretches. "Fuck," he says, just as eloquent. "We agreed not to do this."

"I know," Danny says ruefully. "I fell asleep, I'm sorry."

"It's alright," Noah says with a sigh. "I'll go now, before anyone else in the world is awake."

He dresses in a hurry and leaves Danny with a kiss, and Danny pads into the shower to wash Noah's come off his chest and finish waking up.

The rest of the Europeans goes about as well as Danny was expecting, if not as well as he'd hoped—he comes in a firm second place after Andrei, trailing him by a meager three points. "One day," he says out of the corner of his mouth on the podium. "One day, Lebed." Andrei doesn't say anything, just smiles at the cameras and holds his gold up to his face.

Danny, Noah, and Noemi are on the same flight back to Bern after the competition is over, and they spend it gossiping and drinking the first class champagne. Noah, it turns out, gets handsy when he's tipsy, and Danny spends the second half of the flight with Noah's hand getting higher and higher on his thigh. They can't do anything about it, since their coaches are also on the flight and would notice if they got in the same cab, but it's nice nonetheless, and Danny jerks himself off to the memory when he gets home.

Worlds is in two months, and Danny, as usual, barely notices the time slipping by, so busy is he with training and conditioning. He and Nico reconfigure his jumps in his free program to try and scrape back those points standing between him and Andrei, and he gets the new routine down perfectly with two weeks to spare.

One week out from Worlds, he wakes to find his phone buzzing almost off the table. Blinking blearily at it, he scrolls through text notifications from his parents, Andrei, Nico, and Noemi, and, unexpectedly, some Instagram DMs from Nat. A sinking feeling in his stomach, Danny opens the chat with his parents first.

Mom: Sweetheart, we just want to say we love you so so so much, and nothing on earth will ever change that

Dad: You're our magnificent son and you always will be

Danny: I just woke up

Danny: This is very sweet, but did something happen?

Danny: My phone's ringing off the hook

Mom: Oh, honey

Mom: I'm guessing you haven't checked your Google Alerts yet?

Danny: Oh God

Danny: Tell me

Dad: Danny, honey, you got outed

Danny slams out of the chat window and over to his Google Alerts, heart pounding. And there it is, the first link he sees:

Is Danny Schaer gay? New pics with summer beau suggest that the Swiss heartthrob of figure skating is off the market—for ladies, anyway!

Pictures of Schaer holding hands with an unidentified man and leaving one of Bern's well-known gay bars hit the internet last night. Sorry, ladies—looks like this dreamboat is looking for love in a different direction! (More…)

Chapter 19

DANNY CALLS HIS parents first. "Sweetheart," his mother says, her voice heartbreakingly soft. "Are you okay?"

"I…" Danny is, for the first time in his life, lost for words. "I don't know," he says, defaulting to honesty. "I, I don't—"

"Take a deep breath," his father says. "Everything's going to be just fine, I *promise* you."

"This isn't how I wanted to tell you." Danny's eyes are filling with tears, and he can feel his breath starting to hitch.

"Oh, darling, don't worry about us even a little bit," his mother says. "You could have hired a skywriter and written it in the clouds and we'd be just fine."

Danny sniffles, wiping his eyes. "Is this the part where you tell me you've always known and have just been waiting for me to be ready?"

"No," his dad says. "We didn't know. But it doesn't matter. You're our son, and we love you so much."

"I love you too," he manages before his voice breaks on a scared sob.

"Oh, honey," his mother says, sounding close to tears herself. "Do you need us to come over? We can be there in half an hour."

"I, I don't know," he babbles. "I expect I'll be busy all day, I don't know—" His phone beeps; he pulls it from his ear and looks at it. "That's Nico; we probably have to do damage control all day. I have to take this."

"Go," his father tells him. "Don't you spend a second worrying about us, alright? Just let us know if you need us."

"I love you," Danny says. They chorus their love back to him, and with a shaking finger he switches calls.

"Nico," he says, and then his voice breaks again. "Nico, I'm so sorry—"

"Hush now, child," Nico tells him. His voice is devastatingly kind and soft, and Danny has to grit his teeth against a fresh wave of tears. "You've done nothing to be sorry for." *I will* not *break*, Danny tells himself, twisting his fingers into the sheets. "Are you alright?" Nico asks him. "Are you in danger?"

"I—No, I'm not in any danger." He's still in *bed*. "I'm safe."

"Good. Now, I'm going to come get you in my car, and we'll go to my office, and we'll sort this out, alright?" Nico sounds firm, but still so, so kind. "This is not the end of the world, Danny. This is just a hiccup."

"Doesn't feel like a hiccup," Danny confesses, staring at his clenched-white knuckles.

"That's because you're in the middle of it. But we'll get through this. Just hang tight until I get there. See if you can eat something."

Danny manages a piece of bread, and then opens Noemi's messages, in the group chat with Noah.

Noemi: Oh God

Noemi: Danny, honey, I just heard

Noemi: Are you okay?

Noemi: You're probably busy, or still asleep

Noemi: Call me if you need me

Noemi: I love you so much

Danny: Nico's on his way to pick me up for damage control

Danny: Barely keeping it together

Noemi: Oh honey

Noemi: Nico's a good egg, he'll take care of you

Noemi: Can I do anything?

Danny: Not yet

Danny: I'll keep you posted?

Noemi: Please do

Noemi: I love you so much

Danny: Love you too

Noah must still be asleep, Danny reflects as he opens Instagram.

Nat: I am so sorry

Nat: I swear this wasn't me

Danny: No, don't worry, I know

Danny: Are you okay?

Nat: Oh, I'm fine

Nat: I haven't been identified, and anyway, I'm already out everywhere, I can't be outed *more*

Nat: My company may not be thrilled that I hooked up on a business trip, but we're coming up on busy season and they need me

Nat: Plus, and this is a little selfish, several major sports news organizations gendered me correctly

Danny: Silver linings

Nat: Sorry, I know that's crap of me

Danny: No, it's good

Danny: I would hate it if they hadn't

Nat: You have a good heart

Nat: Anything I can do?

Danny: Do me a favor and don't do any interviews?

Nat: Danny, I know you don't know me that well but I would never

Danny: Right

Danny: Sorry

Danny: Hell of a morning

Nat: It's okay

Danny: Isn't it past midnight in America?

Nat: West Coast. It's only 10pm

Danny: Ah

Nat: I'll keep my trap shut, I promise

Nat: Good luck

Danny: Thanks

Nico rings his bell just as he's finishing up with Nat. Danny buzzes him in and then paces in the entryway until he knocks on the door.

As soon as he's through, Nico sweeps him into a hug. It almost severs the last threads Danny has over his self-control, but he takes several deep breaths, melting into the hug, and manages to keep hold of himself. Nico puts his hands on Danny's arms and looks him in the eye. "This is not the end of you," he says solemnly. "Not unless you want it to be." Danny swallows, wipes his eyes, and nods. "Let's go," Nico says. "We have work to do."

Nico has an old-school conference phone hidden under a stack of paper in his office, and he uses it to set up a three-way call with Danny's business manager and Nico's contract PR person. "Alright," he says, settling back into his chair. "Christina, you first. How bad is it?"

Danny's business manager clears her throat. "We've lost three major sponsors so far," she says, voice even and professional. "You don't have to get a job, *yet*, and the Worlds tickets and fees are already paid for, but unless they crawl back over the summer, you'll be flying coach next year."

"Alright," Nico says. "That's workable. Not ideal, but workable."

"The real good news is, I just got off the phone with a representative from the Swiss Skating Federation, and they're fully behind you." Danny lets out a long breath, some of the tension leaving his body in a rush. "You're their big moneymaker now that Wolf's out of the game, and apparently that's enough to keep them playing nicely. I wouldn't start down the coke-and-hookers route, but as long as you stay in line, you should have their support."

"Not my style," Danny manages.

Nico gives him an encouraging nod.

Jacob, the PR consultant, cuts in here. "There's already been a big social media pushback from your fan base against the website that broke the story for violating your privacy," he says, "and most of what we're seeing from that corner has been supportive. The International Skating Union's been quiet, but your fans are, for the most part, still your fans.

"Unfortunately," he goes on, "we do have to pander to the ISU, and we all know how conservative it is as an organization. I've got a statement all written up for you to put on Facebook and Instagram that will hopefully appease them. Sending it to your email now."

Danny checks his phone, and a second later an email appears.

First off, I want to thank everyone for their support in this trying time. My fans are the world to me, and I never want to let you down.

The story that broke early this morning was a flagrant violation of my privacy. My one desire has always been to skate, and that is what I will continue to focus on. I apologize for the distraction this story has caused.

My focus will remain on doing my best to represent my country at the World Championships. Please continue to show me your support, as you always have.

Danny is shaking his head before he's finished reading it. "Can we take the apology out?"

"Apologies for the distraction are a standard part of any post-scandal statement," Jacob says. "The ISU will expect it."

Remembering Nico's words on the phone this morning, Danny says, "I've done nothing to apologize for."

"I'm not saying you have," the man counters. "But you still

have to kiss a little ass here."

Danny looks at Nico, appealing to him. "Nico, please don't make me apologize for this," he says quietly.

Nico gives him a sharp nod. "You heard the man," he says. "No apology."

Jacob sighs. "Alright, I'll redraft it. Any other notes?"

"Just one," Danny says. "Can we actually use the words 'I'm gay'?"

"You want to?" The man sounds surprised.

Danny nods, even though Jacob can't see him. "If I'm going to be out, I want to be out properly." He swallows, mouth dry. "I'm gay, and I'm not ashamed of it."

"You're making my job more difficult than it has to be," the man gripes.

"That's why I pay you," Nico says sharply. "Make it happen."

There's a revised statement in Danny's email three minutes later. "That's better," Danny says, scanning it. "I like this one."

"Good. Get it on your Facebook and Instagram as soon as possible, then send me your passwords. I'll monitor the comments and delete anything overly hostile. If we can bully the SSF into putting out a statement on your behalf too, so much the better.

"Now," Jacob says, his tone changing a little bit. "This other man in the photographs. Is he a partner? A boyfriend?"

Danny winces. "Just a one-night stand." He opens one eye and looks at Nico. Nico gives him a smile.

"Is he going to be a problem?" Jacob asks.

"No," Danny says, shaking his head. "I've spoken with him and he's promised not to do any interviews or anything."

"And you trust his word?"

"I do," Danny confirms.

"Alright, but if he starts making trouble I'm going to need everything you have on him."

"Thank you, Jacob," Nico says. "Anything else?"

"That's it for now."

"Christina?"

"I'll keep monitoring things, and see what I can do to stop us bleeding any more money."

"Good." Nico nods decisively. "I trust both of you. Danny and I will focus on the skating from here on out." He hangs up and looks at Danny. "You did well," he tells him.

Danny drops his face into his hands for a moment, shoulders shaking.

"You're booked for private ice time today," Nico says. "Do you still want it?"

"*Yes,*" Danny says fervently. He's itching to get out onto the ice, to move and work out some of the anguish he's barely keeping at bay.

"Then get out there," Nico says. "No goals for today, just do what you have to do. Don't push yourself," he adds as Danny picks up his skate bag and stands. "Don't injure yourself."

"Yes, Coach," Danny says. Nico gives him another nod and he heads out to the ice.

Danny works himself to the bone that day, jumping and spinning and dancing until the world seems a smaller, quieter place than it did when he woke up. Nico drives him back home afterward, and he carries the peace from the ice through his shower, until he's settling on the couch with some dinner.

He's almost forgotten about his texts from Andrei, but another one comes in as he finishes up his meal. Taking a deep breath, he swipes it open.

Andrei: Danny, call me as soon as you get this

Andrei: Okay, you're probably busy, but call me as soon as you can

Andrei: Danny. Call me

Danny manages a small smile and pulls up his number. Andrei answers on the third ring. "How bad is it?" he asks as soon as he picks up.

"It's not great," Danny admits. "The SSF is behind me, but I've lost three sponsors."

"I'll fix that," Andrei says dismissively. "Just tell me who dropped you and I'll have them back by the end of summer."

Danny laughs woodenly. "Andrei, even you can't do that."

"Yes I can," Andrei insists. "Get me a list and I'll sort it, I promise."

"Fine," Danny says, throwing his free hand into the air. "Fine, I'll get you a list."

"Now, Daniel Schaer, listen to me very carefully."

"I'm listening."

"You're not allowed to retire."

Danny laughs again, a little more incredulously this time. "I really don't think that's your call, Andrei."

"It's as much my call as it is yours," Andrei says, making Danny snort. "It's my career on the line too."

"Andrei." Danny rubs his nose with his fingers. "You could have a perfectly fine career without me half a step behind you."

"Probably," Andrei says. "But why settle for 'perfectly fine without you' when I could have 'extraordinary with you'?"

"You really mean it, don't you?" Danny asks, a little wonderingly. "You really think you need me."

"I don't say things I don't mean, Danny," Andrei says firmly. "You're not allowed to retire until I do."

"I love you too, Andrei." Danny lets his head thud down on the couch cushion behind his neck. "I'm not retiring," he says quietly. "I'm not done yet."

"Good." Andrei sounds equal parts commanding and relieved. "I expect you to give me your best at Worlds."

"I expect your best, too," Danny says.

"Always."

It's only when he's sinking toward sleep that night that he realizes he hasn't heard from Noah all day. *There's probably a good explanation*, Danny tells himself drowsily. *He'll be in touch soon.*

Chapter 20

DANNY SITS IN the kiss-and-cry, able to do nothing but gape at the scoreboard as his world comes tumbling down around him. Sure, his short program score seemed a little low a few days ago, but that was nothing. Judges are as fickle as children, and there's no doubt he's a little off his game a bare week after being publicly outed. Whispers and stares have followed him ever since he arrived at Worlds. And, of course, Noah's been dodging him the whole time. So sure, he's a little out of it. A third-place finish after the short programs was probably the best he could have hoped for, all things considered.

But clearly the only reason he wasn't lower in the rankings is that he landed all his technical components and didn't give the judges an excuse. Because in his free, just a few minutes ago, he fell on his quad Lutz, and now they've swarmed on him like sharks, taking a much larger bite out of his final score than the error deserves.

He's not going to win. He's not even going to *medal*.

Time goes a little blurry after that. The next thing he's aware of is Andrei, his hands cupping Danny's face as he says something fast and urgent that Danny can't quite make out. Danny shakes his head and knocks him away, pushing past him, desperate to *get out* of the rink that is quickly shrinking around him.

There's a microphone in his face the next time he's aware of his surroundings, and he hears something about *is this the end?* "They're not getting rid of me that easily," he snarls, before Nico's hand closes around his shoulder and pulls him away.

He doesn't come to again until he's in the shower in his

hotel room, hot water pounding his back and neck. He buries his face in his hands and lets out a little scream, before figuring out where in the cleaning process he is and finishing the job. Once he's dried off, he lies on his back on the bed for a long, long time, staring at the ceiling and trying not to think. Eventually, he sighs and reaches for his phone.

He bypasses his Google Alerts—he really doesn't want to see what the media is saying about him right now. Instead, he looks up Andrei, searching for a recording of his performance. It's the only thing Danny regrets not staying for.

"Disgusting, shameful homophobia that should have no place in this sport," World Champion Andrei Lebed spits in post-win interview, referring to his long-time rival Danny Schaer's scoring by the judges.

Danny laughs, a hollow thing that somehow still makes him feel better. He screencaps the headline and sends it to Andrei.

Danny: You're going to get yourself thrown out of this sport

Andrei: Let them try

Andrei: I'll burn the whole thing down before I leave it

Danny: I know it wouldn't just be for me, but thank you

Danny: It means a lot

Andrei: It's disgusting

Andrei: But I'll sort it

Andrei: You're still not allowed to retire

Danny: Don't worry

Danny: Like hell am I going out like that

Andrei: Good

Andrei: You're a fighter

Andrei: I appreciate that about you

Danny: Where did I end up placing?

Andrei: Sixth

Andrei: The bronze medalist was almost in tears

Andrei: He knew he didn't deserve it as well as the rest of us did

Danny: I'm sure he's a fine skater

Andrei: You're a better person than I am

Danny: I think you're a lovely person

They were supposed to stay two more days for the gala and banquet, but Nico gets Danny on a flight back to Switzerland the next day. "I'll stay and do damage control with the sponsors," Nico tells him, putting him into a cab to the airport. "You go home and rest."

"I'm not running," Danny tells him. "This is a tactical retreat." Nico pats his cheek and sends him off with a wave.

He spends the next few days holed up in his apartment, eating food that is not approved even for his off-season and texting with Andrei and Noemi. To his surprise, Vardan calls one night as he's halfway through a pint of peanut butter ice cream. They've kept in touch since the Olympics, mainly through Instagram and the occasional call when their schedules allow. Danny greets him with the first real joy he's felt since his outing.

"I figured your calls of support might be tapering off by this point, so I waited," Vardan says. His low rumble of a voice is inexpressibly soothing to Danny's ears. "How are you holding up, my dear?"

Danny sighs. "Shittily," he admits. "It feels like I got punched in the face and then kicked when I hit the floor."

"I was watching live," Vardan says. "I nearly put my computer through the wall when they announced your score."

"You still watch my events?" Danny asks, touched.

"Of course," Vardan says. "You would watch mine if I hadn't retired, right?"

"True," Danny allows. "Still. Thank you."

"Of course," Vardan says again. They lapse into a comfortable silence for a few moments, before Vardan says, "Are you giving up?"

Danny sighs again, heavier. "I don't know. I said in the moment that I didn't want to go out like that, but if they're going to score me that way for the rest of my career, what's the point?"

"You'll just have to make them score you better," Vardan says. "Give them no foothold for their bigotry."

"Easier said than done."

"I never said it would be easy," Vardan says. "But if you still have love for skating in your heart, it's what you'll have to do. It's what I had to do, when I first came out."

Danny fiddles with a loose thread on the couch cushion under his hand. "I'll think about it."

Vardan hums. "Danny, darling, is there anything I can do? You sound so lifeless; I hate to hear you in this much pain. Not that I blame you, of course, but if there's anything I can do to help, I hope you wouldn't hesitate to ask."

Danny laughs, rubbing a hand over his eyes. "Nothing much to be done, I'm afraid. Unless you feel like flying to Switzerland and giving me a good fucking, like the old days," he adds wryly.

"If I thought you meant it, I would be there in a heartbeat," Vardan says. Danny can hear his smile in his voice, and it makes him ache. "We were quite good at that, if I recall correctly."

"We were *very* good at that, and I'm not likely to have any sex until December," Danny says, not a little bitter. "I can hardly go out and pull, now, and my only local lover hasn't contacted me since I was outed." *That* hurts to say, enough that he regrets saying it as soon as it's out of his mouth.

"Then he doesn't deserve you," Vardan says firmly. "Keep me in your back pocket, okay? If it gets bad, I'll take a sightseeing trip to Switzerland. I mean it."

"You're too good to me," Danny says, a little too earnestly.

Vardan tuts. "A vacation to a beautiful country over the summer to make love to one of the finest lovers I've ever had the pleasure to know is hardly a hardship, Danny. I'd do more for your friendship than that."

Danny brushes away a tear. If his voice sounds a little choked up for the rest of their conversation, Vardan pretends not to notice.

Danny skips Nico's traditional post-season party, opting instead to book as much private ice time as he can afford. Nico doesn't say anything about it, just spots him in silence and lets him be. He has a phone meeting with Christina, his business manager; Nico had managed to keep his remaining sponsors from fleeing at his sixth-place finish, but Danny's next season is going to involve a lot of belt-tightening. He has savings, he'll be fine, but unless one of his lost sponsors comes crawling back, it's going to be a very different experience from this season. Out of desperation, he texts Andrei that list of lost sponsors, and gets back a thumbs-up emoticon.

One day, a week and a half after Worlds, Danny has had enough. He finishes up a block of ice time and settles into the bleachers to catch his breath. He hasn't done any jumps today, so Nico is in his office. Danny is alone when he picks up his phone and opens the neglected text window with Noah. His few feeble attempts at reaching out stare at him, unanswered, from the screen. This time, his first sally gets an answer.

Danny: Okay, this is your last chance to get off the train to Asshole and start being a decent friend

Noah: I don't know what you mean

Danny: Don't play coy now

Danny: You've been avoiding me ever since I was outed

Noah: Not much to say

Danny: How about 'I'm sorry this happened to you'?

Danny: Just a suggestion

Noah: I think we should stop seeing each other

Danny: Yes, you've made that extremely clear

Danny: Is it because you stopped having feelings for me, or is it just that I'm toxic now?

Danny: If the first, you could at least pretend to still want to be friends

Noah: I have to think of my career, Daniel

Noah: You know how heavily my dancing with Noemi relies on the illusion of romance

Danny: And God forbid a straight man comfort a homo after he's publicly outed

Noah: I'm not your boyfriend, Danny

Noah: I never have been

Danny: No

Danny: But you were my friend

Danny: Or at least, you acted like you were

Noah: So because I don't want to fuck you anymore, I'm not your friend?

Danny: Don't twist my words

Noah: It's not like it ever mattered to you anyway

Danny: And what is that supposed to mean?

Noah: Clearly you had no trouble filling your bed with anyone that passed by, despite claiming to have feelings for me

Noah: So it's not like the loss of me in your bed will be particularly devastating to you

Danny: No

Danny: No

Danny: Fuck you

Danny: I offered you exclusivity

Danny: *Twice*, if you'll recall

Danny: And you turned me down both times

Danny: You don't get to turn around and accuse me of, what? Cheating?

Danny: STOP typing

Danny: When you have a proper apology, come back to me

Danny: Until then, fuck off

Danny locks his phone angrily and slams it down onto the bleachers, his other hand coming up to cover his face as the tears come. It starts as a trickle, but soon all the crying he hasn't done since he was outed comes screaming out of his body where it's been lurking in wait and he's sobbing, hysterical and loud. He clutches his hair in his hands and shakes and cries, able only to be grateful that the rink is empty.

Not entirely empty—at some point, he feels a body settle onto the bleachers next to him, and he's pulled into Nico's arms, his coach's familiar cologne filling his nose. Nico holds him until it's done, until he's cried out, limp and wrung dry and so, so tired.

"There we go," Nico says when Danny finally quietens. "I've been wondering where that was."

Danny laughs wetly and pulls out of his arms, sitting back up. "Better late than never?"

"You needed the release." Nico puts a hand on the back of Danny's neck and turns him to face him. "Danny," he says seriously. "I need you to be honest with me. Can you do that?"

"Okay," Danny breathes.

"With the support systems you have in place—with me, and your friends, and your family—do you think you can get through this with just us? Or do you need some help?"

Danny feels his eyes fill with tears again. "I think…" he starts, trailing off before managing to say, "I think I need help, Nico." Another sob escapes him and he covers his mouth with the back of his hand.

"Okay," Nico says, squeezing the back of his neck comfortingly. "That's okay, Danny, I promise. I'll find you someone to talk to. Someone who specializes in gay athletes. And you'll talk to them, and you'll talk to me, and you'll talk to your friends and your family, and together we will get you through this, okay? I promise you, we will get you to the other side of this."

"Okay," Danny says. Pinned as he is, his coach's eyes boring into him, he can't do anything but believe Nico's words. "Okay."

Nico gives him a final smile and a pat and takes his hand away. "Now, I have some news from Christina I said I'd pass along to you," he says. "It'll drive Jacob insane, but I think you'll find it good news."

Danny wipes his nose with his hand. "Tell me."

"ESPN called," Nico says solemnly. "They want you for the Body Issue."

Despite everything, Danny laughs.

Chapter 21

DANNY GOES HOME for a few days, sleeping in his childhood bedroom and letting his father make him meals. Noemi texts him incessantly, aware that something has happened between him and Noah, but he's not quite willing to tell her the details just yet. It's still too raw.

Nico gets him a list of therapists and he calls them down the line, having preliminary phone conversations with each one. He stops when he gets to Dr. Kavanaugh, an American woman with a brassy voice who stops him in his tracks by asking, "In your own words, why are we speaking today?"

Danny stutters to a halt. "Because..." He swallows and tries again. "Something bad happened to me. Two. Two bad things happened to me, in quick succession, and I need some help dealing with them."

"What happened to you?"

He screws his eyes closed. "I was publicly outed at my job, which means potentially the whole world knows about my sexuality. And the man I, I care about, treated me like I was toxic afterward and broke my heart." The words feel like nails coming out of his throat, but there's a surprising relief that settles around him once they're said.

"Okay." Her voice is raspy but calm. "And what do you want to do next?"

He hasn't really thought about that. The whole time since his outing has just been focused on damage control; he hasn't had time to think about what to do *next*. "I just...I want to feel like myself again."

"What would make you feel like yourself?"

"Skating." The answer will always be skating. "But I've been skating the whole time."

"Okay," she says again. "So we need to get you skating in a way that will make you feel more like yourself than the skating you've been doing since it happened. Why don't you think of some things you could try that might do that?"

The conversation moves on from there, but that notion sticks with him—how can he skate differently in a way that will make him feel like himself again? What can he do on the ice that he hasn't been doing?

He keeps talking with Dr. Kavanaugh, weekly sessions over Skype, and in late May he feels comfortable enough to unlock his phone, scroll to the beginning of his last conversation with Noah, and pass it to Noemi while they're eating lunch. Her face grows solemn and angry as she reads, and when she carefully hands the phone back to him, her lips are pursed.

"Are you still going to be able to skate with him?" he asks, worried.

She frowns. "I can skate with anyone. I'm a professional. What I may not do is ever speak to him again." She takes his hand. "But if you're unhappy with me keeping on with him—"

"I'm not," Danny says in a hurry. "Losing his career isn't a natural consequence for being a jerk; and anyway, I'm not ready for *you* to be done yet, and you'd have a hard time finding a new partner in time for next season."

Noemi stabs at her salad with a little more force than the spinach requires. "Just tell me if that changes," she says. "I hereby absolve you of the need to come to any of our skates until he fixes things with you."

"Thanks," Danny says, embarrassingly relieved. "I promise to watch them all on YouTube; I just don't know if I can handle seeing him in person."

"Understandable." She squeezes his fingers. "Are you okay?" Her voice is serious and caring. "I know the thing with him meant a lot to you."

Danny shrugs, able after a lot of work to be equanimous. "I'm in therapy now," he offers. "It's helping. It still hurts, and I'm still angry, but I'll be okay." He smiles at her until she smiles back. "I might get a cat," he adds. The thought has been on his mind a lot lately. He's been feeling the need for more touch than usual ever since everything went down, and he doesn't relish the thought of going home to a totally empty apartment once he leaves his parents' house again.

Noemi lights up. "Oh my God, you *have* to let me come with you," she says excitedly. "There's a shelter near my house I donate to monthly; I'll take you and we'll find you the perfect kitten."

"Okay," he says, grinning. They make plans to visit the shelter the next week. Danny goes home and orders a ton of cat supplies and toys on Amazon, just in case they find the right cat.

To his surprise, a week after he moves back home with a tiny ginger furball he names Marguerite, his manager, Christina, calls him. "Good news," she says briskly when he picks up. "Two of your errant sponsors have come back."

"Wow," he says, scratching under Marguerite's chin. "How'd you swing that?"

"I didn't," she says frankly. "I don't know why they came back. But I didn't want to ask too many questions. I'll send the paperwork over to you to sign tomorrow; send it back with the courier and we'll get it done. They're both better deals than you originally had, too; no need to fly coach next season after all."

When they hang up, he texts Andrei.

Danny: What did you do?

Andrei: Oh, your sponsors are back? Good

Andrei: I expected it to be this week

Danny: Two of them

Danny: With better offers than I had originally

Andrei: I told you I'd take care of it

Danny: What did you do?

Andrei: Never you mind

Andrei: Just use that extra money to buy me dinner next time we're together

Danny: Absolutely

Danny: Thank you

Andrei: Don't mention it

Danny Googles for a while afterward, searching out Andrei's team's press releases, and after a couple of hours of getting tangled in corporate org charts, he thinks he's figured out what Andrei did. It looks like he went two companies back from every sponsor that dropped Danny, and then canceled all his sponsorships with every subsidiary of those parent companies. Within the next few days, he quietly re-signs with the ones that came back to Danny. Danny doesn't quite know what to do with that level of friendship from the other skater, but he resolves to make it worth Andrei's while.

He's starting to get an idea.

"Danny," Nico booms the next time he has private ice time. Sweating, Danny skates over to the boards and takes a long pull from his water bottle. "Do you want to tell me what you're doing?" Nico asks more quietly.

"I'm skating," Danny says.

"You've been drilling triple flips all day." Nico's eyes are boring into him.

Danny shrugs. "It's good to drill the basics every now and again."

"Mhm," Nico says, voice dry. "Do you want to tell me why every single flip has been over-rotated since you started today?"

Danny squirms. "Damn it, lad," Nico says. "You can't try and invent new figure skating jumps without running it by me first."

Danny fiddles with his water bottle. "I was afraid you'd try and stop me."

"Daniel Schaer." Nico pauses until Danny looks at him. "When have I ever tried to stop you doing something you wanted to do?"

He's right. "I want it, Nico," Danny says, his voice low. "I *want* it."

"Then let's get it," Nico says simply. "Properly, and safely. I take it you want it done in secret?"

"I want to surprise people," Danny says, thinking of Andrei. "I don't want them to see it coming."

"Okay," Nico says. "So we'll do it quietly." He puts a hand on Danny's shoulder. "You can do this," he tells him firmly.

"I know I can," Danny says, and believes it. "Thanks."

"Back to it," Nico orders. "Focus on getting more speed in the entrance, and more height in the jump. You'll need both."

"Yes, Coach." Danny salutes him and skates back out.

He lands his first clean quadruple flip in mid-July, and to celebrate, he calls Vardan. They compromise and meet in Prague for a whirlwind five-day vacation, sightseeing during the day and fucking like wild animals at night. It turns out that Danny, with a little extra prep work, can still take Vardan's cock, and the first night they're together Vardan puts him on his knees on the bed and plows him remorselessly, until his face is mashed into the sheets, ass in the air, begging and crying out. They get a noise complaint from both neighbors. Danny has no regrets.

Vardan, delightfully, thought to bring a set of black silk restraints and a blindfold. Danny learns a lot about himself during the hour Vardan sets aside to torment him while he can't do anything about it, lashed to the bed with his eyes covered, able only to writhe and moan and beg. Danny has to kiss him for half an hour after Vardan finally lets him come, Vardan's big hands caressing all over his still-sensitive skin, before he feels able to tentatively stand and wobble to the bathroom for a shower.

"Did this help?" Vardan asks on their last day, their suitcases packed and waiting by the door to go to the airport.

"Not that it wasn't lovely regardless, but did it help?"

"Mmm, immeasurably," Danny murmurs, wrapping his arms around Vardan's neck and pulling him in for a long, deep kiss. It's true; between the sex and the skating, Danny is feeling safer and more settled in his own skin than he has since Worlds. "You're wonderful," he says against Vardan's lips, smiling widely. "I don't know how I would have gotten through this summer without you."

Vardan casually squeezes his ass, making them both laugh. "Danny, darling, it was absolutely my pleasure."

Danny's programs are set by early August, with a spot in the free skate where he can do either a quad Lutz or a quad flip, depending on how he's feeling. He and Nico have managed to keep his attempts to themselves; Danny hasn't even told Noemi, keeping the possibility of landing it at a competition tucked tight to his chest to keep him warm.

He has a wrench of a time choosing what to do his exhibition skate to, but in the end settles on "Bad Reputation." He puts what he'd cobbled together for his other choice, "Single Ladies," on Instagram, and receives floods of *omg who broke your heart* comments, which warm him in a different, angrier way.

He puts the video up on a Thursday, and on Saturday night, his phone rings. Looking at the caller ID, he lets it ring out, settling on the couch with Marguerite to prepare himself. A few minutes later, he gets the notification that Noah has left a voicemail. Bracing himself, he turns it on. The sound of Noah's voice hits him like a physical blow.

"I won't waste your time," Noah starts. "I've been doing a lot of research, ever since I woke up the day after, on how to formulate a proper apology. Everything I've found says it has to have three parts: stating what you did in full, without hiding from it or making excuses; expressing sincere remorse; and saying what you're going to do to make it right. I'll be honest with you; I don't know how to make it right. I've been wracking my brain for months, trying to figure out how I could possibly make it right, and I haven't figured it out yet. But I didn't want to keep you waiting any longer for the first two parts of my apology.

"First, what I did: I let you down. I let my fear of scandal and of losing points and of bigotry drive me to hurt you, when I should have been there to support you instead. You were the best thing in my life, and instead of treating you like it, I acted like a coward. I was a coward, and when you needed me to step up, I let you fall, and I blamed you for it.

"Now for the second part." Noah's voice goes a little wobbly. "God, I—Danny, I don't even know how to begin. I'm so, so sorry, Danny, I'm so sorry, I—" He cuts himself off. Danny can hear him taking a few deep breaths, and when he resumes talking, his voice is a little steadier. "It's the worst thing I've ever done," he says, and Danny has to close his eyes. "I think it's the worst thing I'm capable of doing. And I regret it, Danny. I regret it so much, and if I could undo it, I would do anything. I, I hate mys—" Another pause, another series of deep breaths. Danny is crying steadily now, hand pressed to his mouth, and Marguerite jumps onto his shoulder and butts her little face into his cheek.

"I'm sorry," Noah says, voice raspy with tears. "That's all I can really say. I'm so, so sorry, Danny. You deserved better from me.

"I still don't know how I'm going to make it right. But I will. You don't have to forgive me, you don't ever have to talk to me again, but I will make things right, I promise. I'll try not to keep you waiting long. I'm sorry," he says one last time, and then the voicemail ends. Danny buries his face in one hand, the other mechanically scratching Marguerite under her chin. She purrs, pressing against his head, and he takes a few heaving, gulping breaths and gets himself under control.

Danny: Thank you

Danny: I'll be waiting

Noah: I won't let you down again

Chapter 22

ASSIGNMENTS COME OUT not long after Danny's twenty-second birthday—he's scheduled for Skate Canada and the Bompard. Nico scrutinizes the judge listings for each event and comes to him with a recommendation.

"I say hold onto the flip for France," he says, talking to Danny over the boards toward the end of practice one day. "You won't need it in Canada; the competition isn't as fierce, and I know most of the judges personally. They're a good, fair lot who won't underscore you on bigotry alone. Save the flip for when you need it."

Danny bites his lip. "You really think I won't need it?" he asks, needing to be sure.

"I really do," Nico confirms. "You can clean up in Canada without it, and it gives you extra time to drill before Paris."

"That would come in handy," Danny allows. He's landing the flip about seventy percent of the time in drills, but only about half the time in the actual program.

"Plus," Nico says, and taps a name on the judges list for the Bompard. Danny leans forward and feels his stomach twist. "Recognize him?" Nico asks, and Danny does: It's one of the judges from the panel at the last Worlds.

"Alright," he says. "That settles it. Lutz for Canada, flip for France. I can do that."

"Good," Nico says. "How do the rest of the programs feel?"

"I want to make a change to my step sequence in the short," Danny says, and they spend the rest of his ice time refining little details.

Once again, he and Andrei aren't scheduled for any Grand Prix events together, barring the Final if they both get in. Andrei is set to finish the series early, scheduled for Skate America and the Cup of China; he'll be done by the first week of November. Danny gets a niggling little idea that he subsequently can't shake, and worries over it for a week before finally breaking.

Danny: Hey

Danny: Any chance you can get to Paris?

Danny: I think you'll want to see the Bompard in person

Andrei: What are you planning

Danny: :D

Andrei: What are you PLANNING

Danny: Who says I'm planning anything?

Danny: I just think you'll want to be there

Andrei: Daniel Maximilien Schaer tell me what you're planning immediately

Danny: That's not my middle name

Danny: I thought you loved surprises

Danny: Be there if you can

Andrei: Ugh

Andrei: I'll work on Fyodor

Andrei: It'll be an easier sell if you TELL ME WHAT YOU'RE PLANNING

Danny: I have every faith in your persuasive abilities

To his mingled dread and delight, Noah and Noemi are scheduled to be in Canada with him. He and Noemi have a fashion show in early October to show off their costumes to each other. "God, you're stunning," he tells her as she spins in her free dance dress, a gorgeous deep yellow that stands out beautifully against her dark skin. She beams at him. "What's your theme this year?"

Her face goes a little funny. "Regret," she says carefully. Danny's stomach twists and she frowns sympathetically at him. "I'm sorry," she says, putting a hand on his arm.

He musters up a smile. "It's okay," he says. "I already know he regrets it. Art is allowed to imitate life."

"On the upside, since he's clearly the one doing the regretting, it means I get to look like a snack," she says, a remarkable stab at levity.

"You always look like a snack," Danny tells her. She laughs, and the conversation moves on.

Noemi had kindly looked after Marguerite while he was in Prague with Vardan, and she's agreed to do it again while he's in Paris for the Bompard, but he has to track down an actual cat sitter for Canada, since she'll be there with him. He goes to his vet for recommendations, and winds up cutting a third pair of keys for a vet tech who agrees to look after her. He feels better knowing that the person taking care of her will know what to do if something goes wrong.

Danny kisses Marguerite goodbye on October 24th and Nico drives them both to the airport. "Are you nervous, lad?" Nico asks, looking over at him in the passenger seat.

"No," Danny says honestly. "I feel ready. Prepared."

"Good," Nico says, patting him on the knee. "You are prepared. I'm very, very proud of what you've accomplished this summer, and I have every faith in you for the season."

"Aww," Danny teases. "Are you going soft on me, old man?"

"Hush, child," Nico says primly, and Danny laughs.

Noemi lands in Windsor the morning of the 25th; Danny knows the exact moment she can turn her phone back on, because his buzzes with a text.

Noemi: Dinner???

Noemi: I need my dose of Danny to get me through

Danny: <3 <3 <3

Danny: Not sure I'm up for anything more public than room service

Noemi: Come to mine

Noemi: Dinner on me

Danny: On your sponsors, you mean?

Noemi: You know me SO well

Danny: I'll be there with bells on

Danny: 7 pm?

Noemi: Whenever you like

Noemi: What is time

The two of them stay up irresponsibly late, eating hotel chicken and salads and doing their traditional tallying-up of their competitors' base scores. The night ends with Danny's head in Noemi's lap, her fingers passing softly through his hair. "I hate knowing he's in the same hotel as me," Danny confesses, made honest by jet lag and the presence of his best friend. "I can handle the same city, but the same building is just too much."

"I know, love," she murmurs. "I promise you, it will get easier."

"That's what my therapist says." Danny bites his lip. "But knowing it will get easier doesn't help me *now*."

"Well," Noemi says, "for now, I'll happily play buffer, and he knows good and damn well he has to stay out of your way, trust me. You may have to white-knuckle through being the same building, but you won't have to be in the same room."

"You know what the really fucked-up part is?" Danny asks. "The thought of never being in the same room as him again is almost sadder."

"Oh, honey," she says, still stroking gently through his hair.

Danny closes his eyes and tries to sit with the sadness, the way Dr. Kavanaugh has been teaching him. He sheds a few tears, back in his own room, but when he falls asleep, he's almost at peace with it.

Men's singles are up first, and random order puts Danny in the first group to skate. He's careful to keep any hint of the quad flip out of his morning practice; Nico gives him an approving nod when it's over. He warms up slowly, hugs Nico tight, and remembers that Noemi had mentioned a grueling training day planned for her and Noah, but none of it shakes the certainty, as he takes center ice, that somewhere, through some screen or other, Noah's eyes are on him.

He *has* to do well. He has to prove that the last seven months haven't broken him.

His short program is about Noah. It had to be; he'd had nothing else in his head all summer. It's anger and betrayal and heartbreak, strength and passion. He's spent the past three months in therapy working on how to pull up those first, immediate feelings and harness them safely, without letting them take over again. As he sits in the kiss-and-cry after he's done, looking at his scores, he reflects that he'll have to tell Dr. Kavanaugh it worked.

"Well done, lad," Nico says proudly, ruffling his hair and hugging his shoulders. "Well done indeed." Danny beams at him.

In his room that night, he flicks through the congratulatory texts from his parents, Noemi, and Vardan. Andrei's is waiting for him when he wakes up in the morning, and he answers Danny's reply immediately.

Andrei: Was that what you were planning?

Danny: Who says I'm planning anything?

Danny: But no

Danny: If I were planning something, I wouldn't do it until France

Danny: Can you come?

Andrei: I'm wearing Fyodor down

Andrei: I think he'll let me fly out for one of the events, and back home right away

Andrei: It'll be hellish, so you better make it worth it

Andrei: So. Short or free?

Danny: Free

Andrei: Done

Danny: Assuming you win Fyodor over

Andrei: You've never asked me for anything before

Andrei: I'm going to make this happen

Danny: <3

Andrei: I really won't have time for sex, though

Andrei: That'll have to wait until the Final

Danny: We'll see about that

Andrei: WHAT ARE YOU PLANNING

Nico somehow finds him private ice time across town all day, so he can't pull up Noah and Noemi's short dance until that night. He follows all Dr. Kavanaugh's instructions for self-care first, a long, hot shower, straight into his fluffiest bathrobe. His cat sitter has sent him a video of Marguerite that he saves for after, as a mood boost.

It's still heart-wrenching to watch. Noah and Noemi really are the best in the game, and emotions pour from them like water, evident in every lift and line. He takes a minute to wipe his face, watches the video of Marguerite, and calls Noemi.

"You were stunning," they both say together, and then laugh. "Seriously," Danny says. "You're amazing."

"I cried watching yours," she confesses.

"Same." Danny fiddles with the tie of his bathrobe. "To the point where I'm glad I wasn't there in person."

"The free dance will be easier," she tells him. "It's less...specific."

"I'll still save it for after I go."

"That's probably smart."

The men's free skate is second the next day, just after the free dance. Danny had texted Laurin in June, asking for the most fuck-you gay song the man knew. Laurin had replied immediately, with a smiley face and a song file, and Danny and Nico had built the skate around it. He'll be more motivated in Paris, with the judge from Worlds watching, but he's still angry enough at the ISU to pull off a rendition that nets him a gold medal by five full points.

"Nice to have you back," the bronze medalist, a skater Danny has seen a few times but doesn't immediately have a name for, says to him on the podium.

"Thanks," Danny says, grinning. "It's good to be back."

The reporters swarm him after the medal ceremony. "Nice comeback, Danny!" one says.

"I never went anywhere." He winks.

Another cuts right to the chase. "Danny, who was the other man in the photographs?"

"Now why would I tell you that?" he drawls, raising an eyebrow. "I'd *so* much prefer to keep all your attention on me."

The reporters obligingly titter. "Does it feel good to be back on the podium?" someone else asks him.

"Better than you can imagine," he says honestly. "And I intend to stay there."

Nico pulls him away after another couple of questions. "Well handled," he murmurs in Danny's ear as they leave the rink.

"Thanks."

"I don't just mean the interview," Nico says. The hotel is a block away from the rink, and they step out into the bitter Ontario air and make their way toward it. "I mean this whole summer, this whole fiasco."

Danny smiles at him. "Appreciate it, Coach."

"I don't know what exactly that boy did to you, but I bet he regrets it now." Danny looks at him sharply, wracking his mind for when he might have given Noah away. Nico gives him a sideways smile. "I've known Noah Favre since he was a boy, lad," he says. "It doesn't take a lot to put two and two together, for someone who knows you both as well as I do."

Danny nods, looking down. "He does," he says. "Regret it."

Nico pats him on the arm and they finish their walk in silence.

Andrei: Nicely done on the gold

Andrei: Incidentally, Favre looks more like a kicked puppy than ever this season

Danny: I don't want to talk about Noah

Andrei: Want me to destroy his career?

Andrei: I bet I could do it

Danny: NO

Danny: I already had to talk his dance partner down

Danny: Don't you start too

Andrei: Okay, okay

Andrei: Offer's on the table if you change your mind

Danny: Did you text me just to offer to destroy someone who may or may not be my ex?

Andrei: Not just that

Andrei: Although seriously: On the table

Andrei: Fyodor gave me the go-ahead, finally

Andrei: I'll see you in Paris

Chapter 23

DANNY'S SHORT PROGRAM in Paris goes better than he could have hoped for. Once more he's able to channel his emotions, pouring them all into his skating to earn himself a personal best and a small gold. He's panting for breath by the time the music comes to a close, dripping sweat, but it's worth it to see the score flash on the board.

Nico pats him on the head and hustles him through the post-skate interviews. Thankfully, his performance seems to be drowning out last season's scandal; no one asks him about the photographs, and only one reporter mentions him being gay at all. "I'll take it," he murmurs to Nico afterward.

"No one will ask about your sexuality after your free skate," Nico assures him. "They'll have too many more important things to talk about."

He strips out of his costume in the hotel room, showers, and flops onto the bed to deal with his text messages. Noemi has sent him a string of exclamation points and crying emoticons; to his surprise and amused delight, his father has done the same.

Andrei is already on a plane, set to land tomorrow evening; Danny skates again the day after. He won't have a chance to see Andrei beforehand, as Nico has found him a private rink and ensured the discretion of the staff there for Danny to practice the flip, since he doesn't want to give it away at public practice. Andrei's flight out is at 2A.M. after the free skate, but Danny rather expects he'll make the time to see him before he goes.

Assuming Danny can pull it off. He lands eighty percent of his quad flips at private practice, and tempts fate by doing a few over-rotated triples at the morning public ice time. But he's still nervous, more nervous than he's been before a competition in years. He has to deploy some of the calming techniques he's been working on with Dr. Kavanaugh and flip through his whole Marguerite album before he's able to force any lunch down.

He checks Instagram to see that Andrei has posted a selfie from the bleachers, captioned *Tip-off from a friend that things might get wild today.* He likes the post and puts his phone away, shifting his focus to warming up. Oddly, knowing Andrei is definitely in the audience helps him calm down; his friend has come to see him, and Danny won't let him down.

He's in first going into the free, so he's set to skate last. Nico hugs him as the second-place skater leaves the ice. "You can do this," he says in Danny's ear. "Go make history." Danny squeezes his coach, then swallows and goes out to center ice.

Danny has adjusted his starting pose for this competition. Instead of looking dead ahead, he's turned to the side, making direct eye contact with the judges. As his eyes bore into the judge from Worlds, the man goes pale. Danny smirks to himself, satisfied, and then the music starts.

He and Nico were strategic in placing the flip in this program. It's bounced around various places as they ironed out the details, and they finally settled on just before the halfway point—enough time to gain some confidence with other elements, but not in the second half, when he would be more tired. There's a triple loop-triple Salchow combination before it, and Danny nails it, landing with a flourish.

An Ina Bauer, a camel spin, and then the music builds to an angry crescendo, and there's nothing left to do but swing into his entrance, push off the ice, and leap.

He does it perfectly. Four rotations that he can tell from the air are beautiful and precise; a picture-perfect landing. His ears are ringing even before he jumps, but as his skates hit the ice again and he doesn't fall, he can still hear the crowd *roar* in response. He throws himself straight into the choreography of his step sequence and dances like his life depends on it, biting down a wide grin.

Danny manages to keep his exultation in until the end of the program, but after he drops his final pose, he has to lift one fist into the air, cover his face with his other hand, and shout wordlessly in triumph. The applause is like nothing he's ever heard before, and it goes on and on and on.

He scans the crowd for Andrei as he skates off the ice. Andrei's fire-red hair is immediately identifiable; he's winkled a spot in the front row to watch. The other skater is out of his seat entirely, leaning over the rails with a look on his face like Danny has just offered him an entire cheesecake all to himself, excitement and hunger and delight.

He's also holding his jacket over his crotch. Danny throws his head back and cackles.

Nico meets him with a huge grin and an even bigger hug than he'd sent Danny off with. "Well done, lad," he shouts in Danny's ear in the kiss-and-cry. "It'll be a world record, or I've never seen one!"

It is, as it turns out; Danny now holds the world record for both the free skate and the combined score. "That must feel amazing," a reporter says, holding a microphone to his mouth.

He shrugs, grinning. "You know," he says, "world records never last forever. Scores are beaten every day." In his mind's eye he sees Andrei, already plotting on how to sweep past him in pure numbers.

"But being the first is forever," she says, grinning back at him.

He winks. "Exactly."

"It was a hell of a skate," she says. "I saw that Andrei Lebed is here, on a tip from a friend. Was that you?"

"I thought he might like to see it in person, so yes, I gave him a heads-up that he probably wanted to be here today."

"Do you have any words for your long-time rival?"

Danny looks directly into the camera. "I expect you to have it by the Final, Red Swan."

The reporter laughs. "Alright, thank you for your time."

"It was my pleasure," he drawls.

Eventually, after several more interviews, he and Nico make it out of the rink and back to the competition hotel. "Sleep well tonight," Nico tells him as the elevator stops at his floor. "You don't want to halt your momentum at the exhibition tomorrow."

"Yes, Coach," Danny says. Nico rolls his eyes and gets off.

When Danny arrives at his own floor, he's not entirely surprised to see a figure leaning against the wall by the door. As he approaches, Andrei straightens and flashes a foil square at him. "Hurry up," he says. "I have a plane to catch."

"Told you," Danny says with a smirk, pulling out his keycard.

"Shut up and get in the room," Andrei snaps. Danny raises his eyebrows but obliges.

Once they're inside, Andrei asks, "Bed or wall?"

Danny's pulse jumps and his cock, already swelling, takes an even more decided interest in matters. "Wall."

Andrei backs him up to the wall and pins him with the deepest kiss Danny's ever had from him, tongue sweeping into Danny's mouth without preamble, his fingers flying to Danny's trouser buttons. Danny moans around his tongue and reaches to reciprocate, but Andrei bats his hands away. "We don't have time," he says, diving back in to continue plundering Danny's mouth as one hand slips into his briefs to take a brusque hold of his cock.

"Fuck," Danny hisses as Andrei starts to stroke him, dry and *fast*. "Fuck, Andrei, *yes*."

"Should have known you'd be into this," Andrei says with a grin, before bending his head down to latch his mouth onto Danny's neck just under his ear. "I want to leave a mark," he growls against Danny's skin. "So everyone knows you got what you deserve."

"Fuck," Danny whimpers again, clinging to Andrei's wrist and the back of his head. "Fuck, yes, do it, leave a mark."

Andrei's mouth slips lower, to a spot where it will be half-covered by Danny's gala costume, and starts sucking harder than they've ever dared before, with no small amount of teeth. Danny thunks his head against the wall and swears a litany under his breath, hands tight on Andrei's waist.

Once his cock is hard enough, Andrei unlatches from his neck and drops to his knees. "Trousers down," he orders. Danny scrambles to obey, shoving everything down to mid-thigh. Andrei rips the condom open and slides it onto Danny, and then unceremoniously bends and swallows him as far as he can get. "*Shit!*" Danny yells, clapping a hand over his mouth as Andrei begins to suck him in earnest, one hand wrapping around what he can't fit in his mouth and pumping hard.

It turns out that yes, Danny is *embarrassingly* into this, and it's a bare few minutes of pure overstimulation before he yells again and comes, thrusting his hips into Andrei's face as the hardest orgasm he's ever had rips through him. Andrei rides him through it, gentling only a little as Danny shakes through the aftershocks, and when Danny passes a hand over his hair he pulls free and stands, wiping his mouth with the back of his hand.

"Sure I can't do anything for you?" Danny manages to say, reaching out to paw clumsily at Andrei's hip.

Andrei shakes his head. "No time. My plane leaves in less than two hours." He presses Danny into the wall again with another consuming kiss, and then pulls back and steps away. "See you at the Final," he says, giving him a lustful look that almost has Danny ready for round two, and then he opens the door and leaves.

Danny has to sink to the floor and breathe for a quarter of an hour before his legs are steady enough to get him to the bathroom, but he makes it eventually. He strips the condom off and leaves it in the bathroom trash can, then examines his neck in the mirror. The mark Andrei left is definitely visible already, and he knows from long years of ice skating falls that the bruise will darken significantly by morning. Nico may kill him, but as he presses his thumb against it and thrills with remembered pleasure, he can't regret it one bit.

He showers, then pads to the bed and checks his texts. He has several from Noemi and one, surprisingly and distressingly, from Noah. He checks Noemi's first.

Noemi: GOD

Noemi: You're INCREDIBLE

Noemi: Why didn't you tell me?????

Noemi: God that was sexy

Noemi: I hope you're not answering because you're getting laid

Noemi: You deserve it after that performance

Danny: [img]

Danny: Handled

Noemi: GOOD

Noemi: Go to sleep, you have the gala in the morning

Danny: Love you

Danny: Proud of myself

Noemi: Proud of you too, boy

Noemi: SLEEP

So ordered by his best friend, he locks his phone immediately and falls into a victorious, dreamless sleep. But Noah's text is, unfortunately, still there in the morning.

Noah: Congratulations

Noah: That was an amazing thing you did

Danny: Thank you

Danny: I'm still waiting

Noah: I know

Noah: And I know what has to happen

Noah: I just need a little bit of time to put the wheels in motion, and then I'll finish my apology

Danny: I don't want a public grand gesture

Noah: I know

Noah: I know you, Danny

Noah: Sorry, that was out of line

Danny: Don't keep me waiting much longer

Noah: I won't

Nico rolls his eyes at Danny's neck in the morning, but doesn't say anything. Danny attacks the mark with foundation, but it's just too dark, and eventually he has to give up or use his whole jar. It's mostly covered by his costume anyway, just the barest hint peeking out over his high collar. Probably no one will notice it.

With Noah's texts in mind, it's perhaps the most spiteful rendition of his exhibition program he's ever done.

When he checks the gossip boards after he gets home, there's *plenty* of scuttlebutt about his love bite and who might have given it to him. Sadistically, he hopes Noah is somewhere reading it all.

Chapter 24

DANNY REWINDS THE video again, scrubbing back until the camera is right in Andrei's face and then pressing play. "Andrei, do you have the quad flip yet?" a fan shouts over the noise of the crowd gathered outside the rink.

The shot swims into focus on Andrei's face for the briefest of moments before he winks and says, "Watch and see!" To anyone else, the infinitesimal pause is just Andrei parsing their words over the din of his fans; a moment to turn noise into comprehensible words. But Danny knows Andrei, and he knows what that pause means.

Andrei doesn't have it. Which means Danny might finally win the Grand Prix Final.

"Stay calm," Nico tells him, putting his hands on Danny's shoulders and staring right into his eyes. "This is just another competition, like so many others you've been in. Stay calm, and stay focused."

Danny nods, takes a swallow of water, and shakes his head slightly to clear it before turning back to his warm-ups. But he can't stop his mind from racing. This might finally be his year.

He and Andrei have both won both of their qualifying competitions. Danny has inched his way into the first place spot for the short programs on the strength of his world records, for the first time in his career. Unfortunately, that means he'll be skating last, which leaves him too much time to *think*.

Danny does his calming exercises, stretches his glutes, and keeps his music up loud enough that he can't hear the crowd reacting to Andrei's short program. He keeps his eyes on Nico as he takes the ice, but he can still hear Andrei's score being read over the loudspeaker. It's high, of course; this is Andrei Lebed, and he's more motivated than he has been in years, thanks to Danny's surprise. Of course he would have pushed his programs to the limit.

Nico hugs him, pats him on the cheek, and sends him off. He takes center ice, settles into his starting position, and waits for the music.

All throughout the series, he's been practicing two versions of his short program: One with the quad flip, and one without. For his events in the series, he went for the one without, since just having the flip in his free was more than enough. But now he's competing directly against Andrei, and so he and Nico have spent the weeks since the Bompard agonizing over which version to use.

In the end, they've opted for the version he's been using, without the flip. Up against Andrei, the margins will be tighter than ever; it's the smarter choice to go with safer jumps, and not risk losing points to a fall, which is still all too likely for him with the flip. So when his score comes in a little lower than Andrei's, he's not surprised. But it's close, so close, and with Danny one quad up over Andrei for the free…

"I might actually do this," he murmurs, mostly to himself.

"That's the spirit," Nico says jovially. "Come on, let's clear the kiss-and-cry."

Danny spends the next day in an agony of nerves. He falls on every quad flip he tries at morning practice on his day off, but Nico just shakes his head at Danny's worries. "What matters is how you do it tomorrow," he says calmly. "You're too in your own head today, but you've always been good at settling into the right headspace for the actual competitions. No more jumps today; focus on your spins and step sequence."

He can't bring himself to watch the videos of either of Noemi's dances, which have led her and Noah to yet another Final gold. "I promise to watch them when we get home," he says to her over dinner in his hotel room the night before his free, taking her hand anxiously.

She waves him off. "I know you will," she says. "I want you focused on your own gold. Kick that Russian bastard's ass, alright?" Danny smiles nervously at her, spearing another piece of his chicken.

The day dawns gloomy and cold. Danny has to bundle up more than usual for his walk to the rink, and tries not to take it as an omen.

To his relief, he finds that Nico is, once again, right; by the time practice is over and the sixth-place skater takes the ice, he's much calmer than he was when he woke up. "I'm ready," he tells Nico while the fourth-place skater is performing.

"Are you sure?" Nico asks him, eyes assessing. Danny nods. "Alright," Nico says, and leads him out to continue warming up rinkside.

Danny pulls up the scores on his phone. The other four are good skaters, but he's not surprised to find that no one else really seems to be in contention for the top two spots, based on his and Andrei's base scores. The third-place skater gets his scores, which will probably keep him in a respectable third place, and Danny takes the ice.

All told, his free skate has three quads in it: a toe loop, a flip, and a Salchow, the first and third in combinations. He nails them all, only the slightest wobble coming out of the flip, but he can tell even from the ice that his spins aren't quite as tight or as fast as they have been in practice or the other events. *It's alright*, he tells himself as he dances the song to a close. *It'll keep things interesting.*

Danny does the quickest math of his life in the kiss-and-cry. The score Andrei will need to beat him is technically possible, given his base score, but he'll need to beat Danny's world record to pull it off, with an almost perfect components score. Danny's stomach twists in delighted anticipation as Andrei takes the ice.

Technically, he's supposed to be getting interviewed while Andrei skates, but there's no chance of him giving a coherent answer, so Nico lets him linger to watch instead of hustling him off to where the reporters are waiting.

By this point, Danny knows Andrei's elements as well as he knows his own. He starts with his signature jump, the quad Lutz, and lands it with a flourish. Next is a classic triple-triple, also landed perfectly. Then, just before the halfway mark, a quad Salchow.

His hand touches the ice. Danny's flies to Nico's arm and grips tight. "There we go, lad," Nico says, low and calculating. "There we go."

Danny shakes his read, rapt as he watches Andrei recover himself. He has one more quad left, a toe loop, and he lands it cleanly. "His components look good," Danny murmurs to Nico. "He might still pull this off."

"No way," Nico says, "not with that touchdown—*what?*"

Danny has clapped his hands over his mouth, jaw dropped, no longer listening to his coach or the music or *anything*, because Andrei has turned his last jump, a triple-double combination, into a quad-double, and Danny's chances at gold evaporate in front of his eyes.

Four quads. *Four quads*, in one program. It's unheard of. It's *inhuman*, and yet Andrei has done it. Not perfectly, not cleanly, but he's done it.

Andrei collapses onto the ice when the music stops; Danny is panting hard in sympathy as the other skater slowly pushes himself to his feet to take his bows. "Come on, lad," Nico says in his ear, tugging him away. "We have to get out of his way."

The reporters swarm Danny when he gets backstage. "Danny, before Lebed's scores are read out, how are you feeling right now?"

"Amazed," he says honestly, shaking his head. "I've never seen anything like what just happened."

They're all distracted by the voice coming from the TV in

the corner of the room, reading out Andrei's scores—a new world record, and the gold medal. "Are you upset to have lost what has been your closest competition with Andrei Lebed?" another reporter asks him.

Danny searches himself. "No," he says, a little surprised to find it true. Laughter bubbles up from inside him, and he lets it out, rubbing the back of his head ruefully. "He's a hell of a skater, and I'm honored just to have driven him to the lengths he's gone to today. He's earned that gold medal."

"I want you tonight," Andrei says on the podium through his grin. The bronze medalist looks up at him, startled, and then realizes he isn't the one being addressed and turns back to the cameras.

Danny laughs. "We both have to skate tomorrow," he reminds Andrei through his own smile.

"I don't care," Andrei says. "I want you tonight. Come back to mine; say you will."

Danny looks up at him. Andrei's staring at him, cameras forgotten; the look in his eye is triumphant, gleeful, victorious, and wanting. "Of course," he says. "Champion's choice." Andrei smirks at him.

They stumble into Andrei's hotel room an hour later, kissing and laughing and tearing at each other's clothes. "Well?" Danny asks, giggling breathlessly as Andrei sucks at his nipple. "What do you choose?"

"Oh, I don't care," Andrei says, tugging Danny by the belt loops over to the bed. "What's your favorite sex position? We'll do that."

So prompted, Danny puts Andrei face down on the bed, ass in the air, and pounds into him. From the sounds of it, and the way he's thrashing against the sheets, Andrei appreciates the position as much as Danny had when it was him. "Fuck, fuck me, Danny, fuck me, *fuck me*," Andrei chants, fingers twisting in the bedding, and Danny gives it to him as good as he can. He rakes his nails up Andrei's spine, neck to tailbone, and Andrei yelps and comes with a shudder.

Andrei collapses onto the bed, Danny's cock slipping out of him. Danny takes hold of it and starts jerking himself off, dropping to one hand over Andrei. "You should come on my back," Andrei says lazily, catching his breath below him.

"Yeah?"

"Mhm."

Danny fumbles the condom off, drops it onto the floor, and resumes pulling at himself. "Mmm, give it to me," Andrei says drowsily, looking up at him from behind his fall of red hair, and Danny's balls tighten. A few more strokes and Danny is gone, his come splashing onto Andrei's back, over the thin red lines raised by his nails.

"Fuck." Danny drops onto the mattress next to Andrei, and Andrei turns his head to look at him. "That was a good idea."

"I'm a genius," Andrei says. Danny laughs at him. Andrei smiles, and then places a hand carefully on Danny's chest. "Are you okay?" he asks seriously, fingernail tracing a meaningless pattern over Danny's skin. "With everything that happened, and with losing today. I know you worked hard for that flip."

"It's not losing," Danny says, echoing Andrei's words from so long ago. "It's winning silver." Andrei just keeps staring at him, and Danny sighs, putting his hand over Andrei's on his chest. "I'm okay," he says. "Yes, getting outed was awful, and getting underscored was worse, but it wasn't as bad as it could have been, and I've come back from it." He smiles. "Therapists. Who knew?" Andrei huffs a laugh but stays quiet. "It helps that I have something to my name now that you can't take away from me," Danny admits quietly. "Scores, medals, I'd like to win there, but I was *first* at something, and that means more to me, I've found."

"Good," Andrei says. "I'm glad you have that. You're still the best friend I've ever managed to make, and I'd like not to lose you to gold medal envy." He's smiling, which takes the sting out.

Danny winks. "Still not giving up on the idea of beating you one day," he says.

"It would be a sad day for me if you did," Andrei says sleepily. His eyes fall shut and his breathing evens out. Danny stays until he's sure Andrei is fully asleep before slipping out from under his hand and dressing.

Chapter 25

NOAH: YOU SAID to come to you when I had my full apology. I have it now. Can I come to you?

Danny: 1327

Noah: Thank you

Danny paces his hotel room, taking deep, calming breaths that do nothing to alleviate his anxiety. His Euros silver medal is on the dresser, along with his exhibition costume for tomorrow. Andrei had landed a quad flip by the skin of his teeth earlier that day, assuring himself yet another gold medal.

Noah's timing, at least, is excellent. All that's left is the exhibition. If this conversation goes poorly, at least Danny won't have to compete afterward. If it goes well...

Danny can't think about that possibility.

Finally, an eternity after his last text that is only seven minutes when Danny checks his phone, there's a knock at the door.

Noah has always been the most handsome person Danny has ever seen, and Danny's heart stutters as he opens the door to reveal him, dressed in a button-down and jeans and looking at Danny like he's never seen him before. They lock eyes for a moment, both of them freezing, and then Danny steps aside and motions for him to come in.

Once the door is shut, there's another moment of awkward silence. Danny hasn't seen Noah in person in almost a year, and there's a thousand tiny details to take in: the bags under his eyes, the five o'clock shadow on his cheeks, the twitching of his fingers. From the way Noah's eyes are flickering over his face, he feels the same. Finally Danny breaks his gaze and goes to place himself at the foot of the bed, gesturing for Noah to sit opposite him. "Alright," Danny says once Noah is cross-legged before him. "You've kept me waiting long enough. What's the big reveal? How are you going to make things right?"

Noah takes a deep breath, looks Danny in the eye, and says, "I'm retiring."

The bottom drops out of Danny's stomach. "What?"

"It's all arranged," Noah goes on. "We just okayed the press release an hour ago. It goes out when we get home. Worlds this year will be our last competition; after that, we're retiring."

"You can't," Danny says, not a little bit of panic crawling up his throat. "I don't—what about Noemi?"

"She wants to go back to school," Noah says. "When I told her I thought I needed to be done, she was relieved. I think she knows as well as I do that it's the only option still open for me."

"You *can't*," Danny says again, shaking his head. "You can't be done already."

"I can, and I am," Noah says firmly. "Danny, I would cross the street to avoid meeting the man I've let skating make me into. What I did to you…I want to be someone else, and that means letting competing go. It's time. It's beyond time."

Danny buries his face in his hands. "You can't retire for my sake," he mumbles into his palms.

"I'm not," Noah says. "I swear I'm not. I'm retiring for me." Danny wipes his face and looks at him. "I don't expect you to forgive me," Noah says, eyes holding Danny's gaze. "I wanted to have this conversation in person, but I'm fully prepared for you to tell me to leave and never darken your door again."

"I don't want that," Danny admits, mouth dry.

A complicated series of expressions flash across Noah's face. "Okay," he says carefully. "I can be your friend again, if that's what you want. If you can forgive me enough for that."

Danny shakes his head. "I don't want to be your friend. I *can't* be your friend."

Noah looks confused, and tentatively, painfully hopeful. "Alright," he says slowly. "Cards on the table, then. In your ideal world, if we work everything out, what do you want me to be to you?"

Danny takes a deep breath, closing his eyes so he doesn't have to see what Noah's face does next. "I don't know where you stand," he starts. "But if you still, if you still have feelings for me—"

"I'm in love with you," Noah cuts in. Just like that.

Tears spill out from under Danny's closed lids and he brushes them away. "Fuck, Noah," he says helplessly, rubbing his forehead, eyes still closed. "I want you to be my *partner*. I want us to be together, properly, seriously, a couple. I want you to be my partner, and I want to be yours. I want everything you were holding back when we were pretending to be casual."

Bracing himself, he opens his eyes and looks at Noah. The man is crying now too, tears silently streaking down his cheeks. "That's…a lot more than I was expecting," Noah says shakily. "More than I hoped for."

"More than you want?" Danny asks, wretched.

Noah shakes his head immediately, taking Danny's hand almost unconsciously. "Not more than I want," he says. "Not by a long shot. I want to be that for you."

"Can you?" Danny asks. His voice is thick but he pushes past it. "Great, you want to, but are you actually capable of it?"

"Yes," Noah says. "If I retire now."

Danny groans and covers his face again. He feels Noah's free hand settle, tentative and reassuring, on the back of his neck. "Danny, I mean it when I say I'm not doing this for you." His face is earnest when Danny looks back up at him. "Or at least, not solely for you," he amends. "This is what I need to do, for my own sake. If you can forgive me, if, God knows how, you want me *back*, that's essentially a bonus. A wonderful, miraculous bonus. But I need to retire. I need to be done competing."

It's not enough. It's almost enough, but Danny can't quite believe it. He reaches for Noah without thinking, pulling back before he touches his face. "Noah, I need to—"

"Do what you need to do," Noah says solemnly, and Danny pulls him into a kiss, searching for something, anything, that will let him be sure.

Noah kisses him back. His hand comes up to grip Danny's forearm and he lets out a stuttering, surprised breath, but the press of his lips against Danny's is steady and sure. His lips taste like salt from where his tears have streaked over them. Danny kisses him for a long, lingering moment, and then pulls back to press his forehead against Noah's. "I love you, too," he whispers.

Noah shudders, his fingers tightening on Danny's arm. "That doesn't mean you forgive me," he says, like he's trying to convince himself.

"I know," Danny says. "I know it doesn't." He smiles, warmth blooming through his chest. "But I do."

Noah lets out a sudden, shocked sob. "Oh, Danny, do you mean it?" Danny nods, and then Noah is in his arms, face pressed against his neck. Danny can feel that it's wet as Noah all but burrows into him; Danny squeezes him as tight as he dares. "Danny, I'm so sorry," Noah gasps, clinging to him. "I'm so sorry, I'm *sorry.*"

"I don't need you to be sorry anymore," Danny tells him, cupping the back of his head. "I just need you to be better."

"I will be. I already am." Noah hugs him for a few moments longer, and then pulls back, wiping his face. "I should say this," he says, blinking away tears. "I don't…I don't think I can do it, if you're still going to want to sleep with other people. I don't want to stifle you—" he adds, face beseeching.

Danny shakes his head, taking Noah's hand. "If we're going to do this for real, it would just be us. Just me and you. No one else."

"Are we doing this?" Noah asks. His fingers are tight around Danny's. "Are we doing this for real?"

"I want to," Danny says, a grin he's helpless to stop

breaking over his face.

Noah lunges forward, catching himself just before their faces collide. "Danny," he whispers, "Danny, please," and Danny pulls him in again, catching him in a kiss that's much deeper and more passionate than the last.

Noah's fingers twist into his shirt and Danny breaks away only to reach behind his head and pull it off, tossing it aside as he dives back into Noah's mouth. Noah moans against his lips and leans back, pulling Danny on top of him as they both fumble with his shirt. "Why did you wear *buttons*," Danny says, laughing as his shaking fingers pull them free.

"I didn't want you to think I wasn't taking it seriously by dressing casually," Noah says, and Danny kisses him again. Noah gets the last of the buttons undone and sits up to wrestle his arms out of the fabric. Danny starts kissing down his neck and chest, leaving a wet trail with his tongue as he works at Noah's jeans.

They scramble out of the rest of their clothes, kissing as much as they can. Noah is *worshipful*, running his hands and lips all over Danny's body, relearning him as Danny tries to do the same. "How do you want me?" Danny murmurs when Noah comes up to kiss his mouth again.

"Any way," Noah breathes. "Anything, Danny, *anything*."

"Noah." Danny takes hold of his chin and makes the man look at him. "How do you want me?" he repeats, softer and quieter.

Noah swallows. "Inside me," he says quietly. "Inside me and over me, Danny, *please*."

He's tight when Danny pushes two fingers into him, and his whimpers and broken moans as Danny works him open make Danny press his face against his knee and swear softly. "Fuck, I've missed you," he hisses into the skin of Noah's thigh, slipping a third finger inside him.

"Missed you too," Noah moans, his back arching to press his ass harder against Danny's hand. "God, Danny, you feel so good. Don't stop."

Danny works him open until he's speared on four of his fingers and begging, and then he fishes a condom out of the depths of his suitcase and starts the long, hot press into him. There are tears in Noah's eyes when they're finally locked together. "Are you going to cry the whole time?" Danny teases, to cover the way his eyes are none too dry themselves.

"Shut up," Noah says, laughing, and it's that more than anything that lets Danny know they're going to be alright. "I thought I was never going to feel you again," Noah goes on more quietly, putting a hand to the side of Danny's face. "And it was my own damn fault." Danny takes Noah's hand, presses a kiss to his palm, and starts to move.

Their lovemaking is more vocal than had been their norm, both of them crying out for the pleasure and the relief of being together again. Noah's ankles hook behind Danny's thighs and his fingers dig into his back, urging him faster, deeper, *more*, and Danny gives it to him, fucking him as much and as hard as he can before he feels the familiar clench in his stomach. He braces himself on one hand and reaches between them with the other to pull at Noah's cock, murmuring endearments, so that Noah is the first one to tip over the edge, nails tearing holes in Danny's skin as he wails. Danny follows him a minute later, dropping his mouth to pant hotly into Noah's neck as they catch their breath.

Danny eventually unseats himself, tossing the condom aside and slipping down to plaster himself against Noah's side. Noah's arm goes around him, fingers reaching up to sink themselves into Danny's hair. Danny purrs, realizing in that moment how much he'd missed the feeling. "I love you," Danny murmurs again, just to taste the words.

When he looks at Noah, the man is gazing at him like he's some sort of miracle. "I love you too," he says softly, and they kiss, sweet and tender after their frantic sex.

They lie there for a few moments before the silence is cut by a buzz from Noah's trousers at the foot of the bed. "Ughh," Noah groans theatrically, and Danny laughs and leans away to let Noah sit up and paw at his pockets for his phone. "It's Noemi," he says, tapping at the screen as he wraps himself around Danny again. "Apparently our coach is looking for me." "Send her a selfie," Danny says, snuggling close. Noah flashes him a smile and holds the phone out to snap the picture. He tilts the screen to show the result to Danny. They look exhausted but happy; Noah's eyes are still a little red from crying. "Send that to me too?" Danny asks. Noah kisses the top of his head. "Do you have to go?" Danny adds, a little shyly.

Noah shakes his head as the response from Noemi comes in. "She says she'll make my excuses, and congratulations on getting my shit together." Danny chuckles into his shoulder. "If it's alright with you, I'd rather not go anywhere," Noah says.

Danny tightens his hold on Noah's torso, throwing one leg over his lover's—his *partner's* calves. "Definitely no going anywhere for you, then."

Noah eventually turns out the light and Danny hears his breathing even out, arms going limp and heavy around him. Danny fumbles on the nightstand for his own phone, turning the brightness down so it doesn't disturb him, and sends a series of texts.

Danny: You're really okay with this?

Noemi: I really am, I promise

Noemi: I have things beyond skating I want to do

Noemi: We've had a good run. I'm ready for it to be over

Noemi: And I want you happy

Danny: I am happy

Noemi: Good

Noemi: <3

Noemi: Night love

Danny: Night <3

❖

DANNY: HEY MOM, Dad

Danny: I know you're asleep, but when I get home, there's someone I want you to meet

Danny: Well, you've already met him

Danny: What I mean is, there's someone I want to bring home

Danny: Love you both. See you soon

Danny locks his phone, nestles it next to Noah's on the nightstand, and puts his head on his partner's shoulder, settling down to sleep.

Epilogue

THEY GO TO breakfast the next morning, Danny dusting off their group chat with Noemi to issue the invitation. She twits them for texting from the same room, and they meet at a cafe two blocks from the hotel. "Breakfast is on me," Noemi says, "as a getting-together present," so Danny orders bacon with his omelet and feels no shame at all.

The three of them crowd into a corner booth, stirring sugar into their coffees and chatting more easily than Danny remembers it being. "What are you going to school for?" he asks Noemi. "Physiotherapy?"

She nods. "I got accepted into my top program two months ago. It was *hell* not being able to tell you."

"Sorry," Noah says, and she swats him lightly on the head. "Sorry," he says again, but laughing this time.

"What about you?" Danny asks him, crunching a bite of toast. "What are you doing after Worlds?"

Noah opens his mouth to answer, but Noemi cuts in before he can speak. "He's going to be a *commentator*."

"Really?"

Noah blushes. "The SSF and I are still working out the finer details," he says, swallowing a mouthful of breakfast sandwich, "but yes, it looks like it."

"Wonder if they'll let you commentate men's singles," Danny muses.

"I'll have to ask," Noah says. "I can be objective."

"'And there's Schaer's signature quadruple flip, *objectively* the sexiest move in men's singles skating,'" Noemi drawls in a passable imitation of Noah's voice. Danny laughs so hard he almost snorts coffee up his nose.

"I don't sound like that," Noah says primly.

"You do," Danny and Noemi say together, and then burst out laughing again.

Over Noah's shoulder, Danny sees the door to the cafe open and a familiar figure step inside, flipping a hood off fire-red hair. Andrei takes a second to look around the place before his eyes land on Danny. They then flick to Noah, and back to Danny, a clear question on Andrei's face. Danny nods, aware that he's beaming slightly and not inclined to fight it.

Andrei smiles at him, a big, warm-hearted smile, and just like that their friendship shifts, the sexual aspect coming to a close in the middle of a cafe in Zagreb. Danny's not worried, though; whatever comes next will be just as fun.

Noah looks over his shoulder and sees Andrei. To Danny's surprise, he beckons at the spare spot at their table. Andrei raises his eyebrows but nods, places his order, and joins them, Noemi shifting down the bench to make room. "Did you all find this place from the same Yelp review I did?" he asks, unwinding his scarf from around his neck.

Noemi shakes her head. "We just wandered until we found somewhere. Why, are the reviews good?"

Andrei answers, but Danny can't quite focus on his words, because under the table, Noah's hand brushes his. His pinky finger reaches out and locks itself around Danny's, and the expression on his face when Danny looks at him is quietly glowing. Danny smiles into his coffee cup and tunes back into the conversation.

T.J. BLACKLEY IS a bisexual queerling with all the gender of your average river rock. During the day they live in the library, cataloging as many books as they can get their hands on, and in the evening they come home to their beloved cat and write as much queer romance as they can think of.

For more information, visit tjblackley.com.

68703104R00109